NEXT LEFT

AND
OTHER STORIES

ASH ERICMORE

Written by: Ash Ericmore

Copyright © 2023 Ash Ericmore

Cover: Grim Poppy Design

All Rights Reserved. This is a work of fiction. No part of this publication may be reproduced, distributed, or transmitted in any form or by any means, except in the case of brief quotations embodied in critical reviews.

ISBN: 9798863471174

WITH SPECIAL THANKS TO

CHRISTINA PFEIFFER, AUGUST VAUGHN,
JESSICA SHELLY, DONNA LATHAM,
CRYSTAL COOK, KIMYONA DIETTER,
CHRISTOPHER RIDGE, UGUR KUTAY, NAT
WHISTON, EDDIE GREENHAM, ERICA S,
CAT GOY, AND EMMA BUTLER

ILL REPUTE

CULT KILLING MONSTERS

NEXT LEFT

THIS ONE DOOR

HATCHING

ILL REPUTE

ASH ERICMORE

ILL REPUTE

ONE

"Come on, come on." Ralph waved Donnie towards the door, but Donnie just sat firm on the stool. He didn't want the both of them to go. It was a stupid idea. He looked across the pub to the crowds of fucking people. Since this fucking pandemic had eased up and everyone was allowed back in the pubs, everyone was *in* the pubs. Friday night, man, just like the old days. Ralph had now pushed himself almost out his seat. He had his hand on his packet of smokes on the small table, tapping it, agitated. The two of them were huddled in the corner of the place. Not a seat remained in the house. Pox-arse small table. Two stools. Just big enough for their pert pretty arses to hang over.

"I want a smoke," he said.

Donnie shook his head. "Fuck no. Go and have your fag—but if we both go, we'll lose the table."

Ralph finally stood, taking his glass up with him and downing it. He all but slammed the empty pint on the table. "There," he said. "Come *on*." He had a sway to him. Had a skin full.

Donnie took his pint and stood. "Where do you want to go from here?" He turned, wending his way through the punters, arm out in front, glass leading the way, like a beacon, through the sea of leather and lace. He looked at a couple of the girls as he went, shaking his head. Legal enough to get it, but not for him.

"I've got a plan," shouted Ralph over the noise.

Donnie shook his head, got to the door and out. The night air, brisk. Slapping him in the face. February. A shitty time of the year to be out on the lash. He stood away from the other smokers, shoulders hunched, and waited for Ralph to follow out. He did, nodding at the other smokers and then came to Donnie. "I don't know how you can still afford that shit," Donnie said, gesturing at the pack.

Ralph looked at him over the light, blazing in his cupped hands. A slight smirk. Something darker, maybe. "Each to their own." He drew hard on the smoke, the cherry flaring in the cold night.

"So what? Home?"

"Nah. I wanna get laid."

Donnie blinked at him. "Right." He looked over to the others. No one paying attention. Then he straightened his jock and continued, "Well … you know I'm not like that."

Ralph snorted.

"We should have stayed inside. Did you see that lot in there?" They may not have been to his taste, but if Ralph wanted to get laid …

He was watching Donnie. The smirk not moving. "I have a better idea."

Donnie sipped his beer. The first and only alcohol of the night for him. Designated driver and all. "A better idea," he whispered in echo. The last time Ralph had a better idea Donnie had picked him up from outside the nick at ten in the morning. The following day, when Ralph had a black eye, had lost his brother's leather jacket, and looked very, very pleased with himself. "Go on."

"You're still all right to drive, right?"

Donnie looked at his beer. "Yeah." The word came from him like a dull wind. He didn't really want to spend a night in the cells.

Not for one of Ralph's ideas.

"Take a left here."

Donnie pretty much scowled into the steering wheel. He'd had about enough of this. Not only had Ralph smoked in the car, he'd also made him drive a good four miles out of the town. He was on the main road now to the city. "Where?" he hissed. He was about ready to turn the car around and go back to town. Drop Ralph off at a bus stop. That would show him.

"Up here, on the left."

On the left. They were on a fucking dual carriageway. There was *only the left*.

Even though it was dead of night now, the dual carriageway still had a good number of cars on it. On the left, up ahead was a house. A house that Donnie had driven by a hundred times. It looked lavish. Always had done, and he'd always assumed it was some country club or a hotel of the elite or something. Ralph was eager for the two of them to drive up the expansive driveway to the house, stood on a hillock, towering over the road. The lights on, breaking the blackness of the night sky behind it.

Shit. He was going to regret this, wasn't he?

Donnie pulled off the carriageway into the drive, slowing. "This had better not be a fucking joke," he said quietly.

"When have I ever let you down?" Ralph was leaning forward in the passenger seat, holding his seatbelt away from his chest. Still slurring. He shivered. "Mind if I put the window back up?" When Donnie shook his head, silent, more interested in the driveway and why the fuck they were there, Ralph pushed the button and the window went up, trapping his smell in with them. Stale cigarettes, and spilled beer.

"What are we doing here?"

Ralph popped the seatbelt, and let it rewind over him, on private land now. "This, my friend, is where dreams come true."

TWO

The driveway led to a circle outside the front of the building. Like in the old movies, where a horse and carriage would come in one side and back out the other. A few cars dotted around it. Parked. Expensive cars, too. Merc. Rolls. A couple of sports cars that could have been anything. Donnie didn't know shit about cars, but what he did know is that his motor did not fit in well there. Banged up on one side—which wasn't his fault, but because he was still in his twenties the insurance company had pushed back on—old Ford. Reliable as fuck. He'd been sold on it. Never wanted anything else.

He pulled into one of the spaces and looked in the mirror through to the building, now behind them. "You *have* to be yanking my chain," he said. "Are you trying to get us in the shit?"

Ralph pushed his hand into his pocket and wriggled about, before pulling his wallet. He opened it up, and started fingering through the business cards in there. The leather was stretched, the wallet a thousand years old. Busting at the edges with cards, and coins bulging the bottom of it. And, Donnie noted, bursting with fucking notes.

"What the fuck have you got all that for?" Donnie looked at Ralph who had stopped rummaging. He was returning the look, grinning like a wild man.

"Here." He pulled a business card from the wallet and pushed it at Donnie. Donnie took it and held it to the window where the lights of the front of the house made it legible.

"That's this place, right?" There was no doubt in Ralph's voice. He was simply punctuating that they were where they were supposed to be.

It was. Donnie looked at the address. There was a gold embossed image of the house on the front, above the address. He flipped the card, the rear blank. "And?" he said. But Ralph already had the car door open and was climbing out.

Donnie got out, and hissed after his friend. *Friend.* "Hey." But Ralph was already halfway between the car and the front door. Donnie rushed after him. "What the fuck are you doing? Why have you got—" As soon as Ralph's foot touched the five stone steps to the front door of the house the light above it came on. Enough to stop Donnie. He slowed to a pause, watching as Ralph climbed up, looking up the outside of the house like he was in awe.

The pearly gates or some shit.

Then Donnie started up again, running to catch him before he made a fucking fool of himself. He got to the bottom of the steps, just as Ralph reached the top. His hand up. Knocking.

Fuck.

Donnie stopped there. Waiting for some bozo butler or a doorman or something to open up and threaten them with the police. He'd just about had enough of Ralph, to be honest, and this was the end of it. The end of the line. The end of his wick. What. The. Fuck. Ever.

Then the door opened, and Donnie's mouth

dropped, a little, open.

It was a woman. Not a girl. Couldn't call her a girl. She was probably forty? Yeah. He was going to go with forty.

Hold on.

His brain was still processing. She was wearing a silk gown thing. A kimono. Something like that. Japanese robe. Silk. No one was saying anything. Why was no one speaking?

Maybe Ralph was staring at her in the same way he was?

Mouth open.

"Boys," she said. Then she slipped to the side of the door and Ralph stepped in.

Donnie watched him go. Disappearing in. Then he was stood there alone. At the bottom of the stairs. What the fuck was going on? She came back. She was stunning. Like movie-star-stunning. Slender, but not thin. Hourglass. Long brown hair. Straggled out like she'd just gotten out of bed, but had a stylist there, just to make sure that whoever she was in bed with, wasn't about to get out. The robe hid a lot of her proportions, but Donnie's mind was awhirl and she was perfect. In almost every way. She brought her hand up and beckoned him forward without speaking.

Donnie realised he was standing there staring at her in silence.

In all fairness, when you looked like that, you were probably used to it. Must be a nightmare trying to go around the supermarket.

Who was Donnie kidding? This woman didn't go *shopping*. She didn't need to. He'd do it for her. If she wanted. Like every week. Just so long as she smiled at him when he brought it over. He drew air in. Followed Ralph up the stairs and went in. He tried not to keep staring at her.

But it was *hard*.

———

Ralph was stood in the middle of the open entrance hall. Donnie looked around, attempting to keep his eyes from his host, not wanting to seem rude. There was a marble staircase winding off, up, the walls adorned in pictures of people. Donnie expected them to be of crusty old men—as was the nature of rich houses to have, but as he looked from one to the other, he found they were of beautiful people. All, so beautiful. Men, women, and a spectrum of the in between. Eventually his eyes dropped to the woman. She was standing, the door now closed, watching the two of them. A glint of glee behind her eyes. "Good evening," she said. She stepped forward, and Donnie caught a glimpse of leather beneath the robe. Boots. He could feel himself getting a little light headed. He glanced at Ralph, his attention fully on the woman. Why hadn't he prepared him for this? *Christ*. This was a whore house, wasn't it? He realised he still had the card in his hand, long forgotten. He brought it up and looked at it. All these years he'd driven by the place and it was full of women doing things for money. He could feel his face, burning a crimson red. "And what can we do for you tonight?" Her voice broke Donnie from his thoughts, and he looked up at her.

"Oh," he said, but before he could collect enough thought for a sentence, Ralph cut in.

He stepped forward pulling his manky wallet from the folds of his jacket and dragging out all the cash. *All* of it. He knew. He knew the prices. He knew how much to bring. He thrust it forward towards the woman. "Everything," he said.

She took the pile of cash from him, barely giving it a glance. "Not a problem, Sir." She smiled, almost subserviently. She stepped to the telephone table—Donnie shook his head. Telephone table? Fucking hell. Like a house like this would have a telephone table inside the front door—and took the small bell from it. She shook it and a trill ring danced through the hollow of the hallway. A slight sound from the floor above and then the clack of heels on marble. A woman came down the stairs. She was younger than the woman that answered the door. Donnie had, by this point, collected enough thoughts to then assume she must have been the madam. But he'd seen a lot of American movies. Did they have madams in England? *Fuck*. Most everything he knew about English prostitution was that it was either trafficked, or crack whores. It probably wasn't but that was the media's interpretation.

The woman came down the stairs and collected Ralph. She was stunning. Donnie was a little jealous. She wore a tight wrapped dress. Showed off her form. Her figure. She was made up. Together. She looked like a princess. The two of them returned to the stairs and without word started climbing.

"And you?" the madam continued.

Donnie turned to her. "Fuck," he whispered. "Do

you take card?" He didn't even know how much was in his account.

She giggled. It was the single most attractive thing he'd ever seen. A glance to the girl with Ralph. These women were ... *perfect*.

"Your friend has paid for you both," the madam continued.

Donnie glanced to Ralph. He was standing on the stairs, waiting for the look. He finger gunned at him.

Finger gunned.

"Go for *everything*," he said. Then he and his counterpart continued up the stairs.

Donnie returned his look to the madam. "Everything?" he said, dryly.

She smiled. The room lit up. And she rang the bell again. "Good choice," she said.

The sound of Ralph disappeared into the echoes of the house, and the sound of another set of steps filled the void. A woman came down the stairs. She was wearing a cocktail dress. She slinked like a cat when she walked. Donnie could almost hear her purring. She reached the bottom of the stairs and went to him. Reaching out and taking his hand. He glanced back to the madam, another flush of red. Like he'd wished she could have taken him. An older woman, yes. That was very much up his street.

You know, if he could choose, like.

The woman led him to the stairs and they climbed. Donnie whispered, "Hi, I'm Donnie." She looked at him without stopping her gentle motion, like the smoke from a candle drifting in a breeze. She smiled, and looked away. Almost embarrassed for him.

He'd never done this before. Were you not supposed to introduce yourself?

Three

The room they'd ended in was pleasant. It wasn't what he was expecting. Having never done this before—no, that wasn't a lie—he could only expect the sort of things you saw on something like ... oh, I don't know ... NYPD Blue. Some place Sipowicz would kick the door into and wave his strangely small gun around. The sort of room you could catch something from, even through the TV.

No, this looked more like a hotel room. Like one in the Business District. Overpriced. But it smelled nice. That was something. She'd led him to the bed and sat him down, smiling demurely at him, before turning and leaving. Again, without fore-knowledge of proceedings he wasn't entirely sure what was going on, or indeed what his so-called friend had told him to order. For all he knew this was some upscale restaurant experience and he'd gotten completely the wrong end of the stick.

The door to the room opened again, and another woman returned. Someone *else*. Right. Was he supposed to introduce himself to this one, he wondered? She turned to face him, closing the door behind her.

She was stunning.

Somehow *more* stunning than the madam. Donnie squirmed on the bed a little. Fuck. He was just sitting there, listless. Was he supposed to ... oh God, he *didn't know*. So he sat there like a plum. Purple, but soft. "Hi," he whispered.

She came to him, across the room. She flowed. A gown behind her, deep red, translucent in the warm glow of the lights. Below the silken materials was a body he'd die for. She was older than the woman who'd brought him to the room. Mature, but with a softness on the skin he could see between ties of lace. The robe covering only black undergarments more complicated than he'd ever been privy to before. The thought briefly crossed his mind that he had no idea how to get that off, and if this was a restaurant experience—which he was now doubting—their wait staff must get quite cold.

That was when he started to giggle.

Couldn't help it.

She came to him. Motherly in stature, but oozing sex. She filled the room with need. He *needed* her. He *wanted* her. It wasn't something he could explain. She filled his very desires, his fantasies. Her face china smooth, eyes deep and full of life.

Oh.

She rested her fingers on his lips, stopping the giggling. Leaning forward, she placed her lips on his. He didn't close his eyes. Like he would have with almost anyone in the world. He didn't want to *not* see this. She looked back. The two of them entwined in a gaze together. Her hands slipped down his body, and he could feel her probing his torso through his clothes, gently, before she stood and dropped the gown from her shoulders. Dropping it to the floor behind her.

Donnie was suddenly very focused on his breathing. Her body was perfect. He couldn't believe someone that fulfilled his fantasies actually existed, let alone was standing there, half naked in front of him.

"Oh, fuck," he said. Blurted, really. He was on the cusp of blacking out. Which wasn't sexy. He knew that. He wasn't really experienced, of course. No idea what he was doing. But he knew enough to know what went where, and he wasn't a virgin, so that was something. Although he probably shouldn't be too worried about impressing this woman with his sexual prowess. She probably didn't care all that much, did she?

She pushed him, gently, back onto the bed, flat. Pulled at his belt, opening his jeans while he watched. He realised he was hard in there. Already. She was opening his fly. He wanted this to last, and she seemed to be moving far too quickly for him. He tried to rise, to sit up. So many thoughts rushing through his head. He wanted to see her. All of her. He wanted to touch her. To suckle on her.

Her hand came up, stopping him. There was a force behind her touch, not enough to force him to stop, but enough to assure him that she was in charge, and he certainly shouldn't be worrying his pretty little head about what was going on.

Just be there for the ride.

His jeans pulled open, she pushed his shirt up his body, a small patch of hair visible above the line of his shorts. She leant her head down to the base of his stomach, her ruby lips caressing his skin, smooth and hot, he could feel her movements over him as he rested back, looking at the ceiling. She expertly avoided touching his cock.

He was worried that she might not have to touch it for very long, as his whole body began to burn at her touch. "Fuck," he whispered. Watched her stand, there in front of him, removing the rest of her clothes.

She stood, naked. Her breasts heavy. Hair unkempt below where her panties were. She reached down and pulled his jeans down, hard, his boxers at the same time. His cock jerking out, free. She sucked air in through her mouth, all but closed. The sound of pleasant surprise.

Donnie looked down at himself, half expecting *someone else's* to be there, having never had that sort of reaction before. She crawled onto him. Hands sliding up the inside of his shirt, until she had it high enough to remove, slipping it over his head. He looked down at her, on top of him. His cock, when it flexed it brushed against her pussy, and he could feel it, wet. Rising, she slid up, straddled across his chest. He could smell her. Fragrant and wanton, she took his wrists guiding his hands to her breasts. Donnie felt them, fat and warm. Soft. Her nipples hardening. She breathed hard like he was some fucking Fabio, and her heart beat harder.

She whispered, "Oh, God, please," pushing herself up his body further until her wetness was close to his mouth.

Donnie couldn't believe that anyone would be doing this. Not *this*. This was all he'd ever wanted. Since he was a very young man. His tongue lapped against her, her thighs tightening on his head as she ground into him, letting him in, deeper. Her sweet flavour of cherry on his tongue, Donnie delved harder, looking to find that spot inside and make her come. He wanted her to come over him. Gush. Revel in his performance, and make him complete.

She reached around behind her, stroking his cock to

edge as she squealed out in pleasure. Releasing him before he had a chance to come himself, as her squeals became screams and she came, her juices flowing hard out, into his mouth as he lapped them from her. Tasting her sweet, tender essence. She pulled back, shuddering, breathing hard, away from him. His smile, broad. "You're amazing," she said. Rolling to the side, breathing like she was exhausted. She took his cock again within her fingers and stroked him. Flexing as she brought him close, but releasing him before climax. "Never have I ..." she said, the words drifting off like she wasn't sure what to say. "... I need you," she continued. She straddled him. Feeding her fingers into his mouth, feeding her juices slicked over his skin in, as she took his cock and drew it inside her.

Her heat surrounded him. He could barely breathe with ecstasy. His urge to come rising hard and fast. He tried to pull out. To move away. He wasn't ready. He didn't want it to end. But she bucked on him. In control. He wanted to stop her, but he didn't want her to relinquish the power. It was what they both wanted. He *knew* that.

So he rose to meet her, joining her rhythm. The burn of orgasm rising from his back, he started to shudder as he came, spurts coming from him, without thinking. He slowed, as did she. But she didn't slide from him. Holding him deep inside her.

"You're amazing," she said. "So good."

Donnie smiled. He *felt* amazing.

The two of them basked in the glow for long moments, their breathing slowed. Then she slipped from him, releasing his cock, softening and sticky, getting from the bed. She took a container from the bedside cabinet and placed it next to his body on the bed. "Eat," she said, quietly. "You'll need your strength."

Donnie pushed himself to one elbow. A Tupperware of cherries. He thumbed the lid off and took one into his mouth. Stoneless. Watched her watching him. His cum drooling down the inside of her leg. She didn't even acknowledge it. He roamed her body with his look. Wondered what she was thinking as he popped the fruit into his mouth. Keep his strength up? He smiled to himself. Wondered what that meant. He could feel his cock flexing. The blood returning. Quick, too. He was used to having to wait at least thirty minutes before his body was up for it again.

As soon as it moved, she did. She came back to the bed, and climb on, ignoring that he still had a hand in the pot of cherries, and she hungrily slipped him into her mouth, bringing his cock back to full hardness quickly. Donnie started to laugh. "Easy there," he said. "Give me a minute."

Without removing him, she looked up, met his eyes. She shook her head. No. He wasn't getting a minute. But apparently he didn't need it. She was already working his cock well enough that it was rock hard. Ready to go. She held it by the root and took it from her mouth, manoeuvring herself onto him, never letting it go.

Donnie felt the cold of his cum as she straddled him again. It dribbling over her.

He felt himself recoil. "Couldn't you wipe that up?" he said.

She ignored him. He was already being fed into her. Her heat again surrounding him. The feel different with her slicked in his fluids. As she started to gyrate on him again. Hand pushed on his chest, forcing him back onto the bed again. Her breasts hanging pendulous over his torso as she rocked against him. "Come in me," she said. Pleading. "God. I want you. I *need* ... you."

As masterful as a man Donnie's age thought he was in bed, he didn't feel like this was right somehow. His eyes were, however, glued to her perfect body. The feeling of having his dick double dipping in his own love-juice now gone. He could feel something orgasmy rising once again. He removed his hand, hanging listless in the cherries, and reached up, taking a breast in each hand. His thumbs running over her hard nipples.

A sickness in his gut. Woozy, sea sickness.

Ignoring it, he squeezed, feeling her perfect body. His eyes hanging heavy as the orgasm gripped him. "I'm going to come," he muttered. Trying not to lose his way. No woman wanted a man who couldn't stay awake after, and this would be much worse, right? His gut turned and a burning sensation started to run up his throat. Bile looking for exit. Donnie tried to get himself to his elbows, but she pushed him down. Fucking him harder. She started to rotate her body, squeezing his cock with her pussy. The burning up in his mouth, choking him. He tried to speak but couldn't.

Orgasm rushing out of him, as he coughed vomit out over his face.

Her look never changing, a mixology of want and pleasure and desire and greed. His cum rising from him, into her. Bile burning his face as he shuddered in pleasure.

Before the blackness …

Four

Donnie woke. Eyes closed. He was cold. Stiff. Trying to swallow the dank taste of the morning after from his mouth, the pain in his throat stopping him. Nose hurt. Inside. Like when he was breathing. He made a mutterance and pain racked him. Felt like man-flu. He snorted a laugh, couldn't help it. Wait.

Where the fuck was he?

He opened his eyes in the dark. Cold. He was on his back. Flat. Didn't feel like a bedroom.

"Donnie?"

He recognised the voice, but it seemed so far away.

"You awake, man?"

"Where am I?" He tried to move his hand to bring it up to his head, but he couldn't. He was weak, sure, but not that weak. Something was stopping him. Trying to turn his body. No. He was restrained. He blinked. Braced himself. And then lifted his head. Looked down his body.

Through the darkness he could see he was naked. There was dirt or something on him. Things … dried. "Ralph," he muttered. "Where the fuck?" He looked to the side. Ralph was there. Next to him. He was on a fucking gurney or something. He looked like he was belted down like a mental patient. His eyes opened wider, a sudden pang of realisation, a stroke of fear. "What the fuck happened?" The words came gruff.

Throat sore. He remembered. He was fucking that chick. No. No, she was fucking him. She wasn't stopping. And he was throwing up.

Was that why he was there? Some sort of twisted revenge for him chucking up on himself in the middle of a bout of passion with a prossie? He looked down Ralph. He was also naked. "Did you throw up over your whore?" he asked.

"What? No."

The two of them met eyes. Ralph looked tired. His skin didn't look right, like he'd been neglecting himself. In all fairness, he probably had. Donnie really should get him into rehab or something. Make him take a bit more care of himself. Although, since when did Ralph ever listen to him?

"Did you?" he asked.

Donnie frowned at him. "No," he lied. "Where are we? What the fuck is going on?"

Ralph looked away. Turning his head back to face the ceiling. He ignored the question. "Cold," he said.

Donnie was aware of the coldness. It was the *strapped to a gurney* thing he was more interested in. "*What's going on?*" he hissed.

Ralph snapped his head back to face him. "I don't know," he barked.

"Tell me what happened to you. You went upstairs with that girl. Then what?"

"Well ..." Ralph looked back to the ceiling like he was at a campfire about to tell a story. "She took me up to this room. It looked like something out of an old

Victorian whorehouse. Proper Sweeny Todd shit. And then her friend came in and the two of them started kissing. And then they started to undress each other while I was watchin—"

"—I don't need a blow by blow."

"That came later."

"Cunt," he whispered.

"This isn't my fault."

Donnie shook his head. "You can skip to the bit where you ended up on a gurney strapped up in a basement." His throat burned with every word. Swallowing was worse.

"Well. After they'd …" he voiced drifted off for a moment like he was fast-forwarding a porn film in his head, "… I'd finished, but the second one wanted more. I mean, who am I to argue, but I didn't think I was going to get it up. They fed me—"

"—cherries."

"Yeah. How did you … anyway. I guess it was all too much for me, and I blacked out."

Donnie was tapping his head back on the gurney, thudding it lightly against the metal, like it might help him think. "Yeah," he said quietly. "Close enough."

"What are we doing here?" he said.

"You brought us here, you must have been here before."

"Nah … bloke down the pub told me."

Donnie looked at him. Frowning. "Bloke down the pub told you? When?"

"Lunch time. I was in with a couple of guys from work for a swift half and I got talking to this geezer at the bar. He passed over the card. Told me to order *everything*. And to bring a friend." As he spoke the words got slower. "I was set up, wasn't I?"

Donnie started to thrash, but the straps were too strong. Honestly, if he could have just gotten to Ralph he could have strangled the fucking life out of him, and then been a good boy and gotten back on the gurney. Killing Ralph now *would have been enough*. "Fuck," he said, stopping, the straps cutting into his flesh. "Fuck."

"Damn," said Ralph. "Man. You think they've robbed me?"

"What of? Your clothes?" Donnie looked around the darkness, squinting to try and see something. Anything. Nothing but vague shadows surrounded him.

"I mean, the money. But I got fucked."

"We both got fucked," Donnie agreed. "See if you can get free." He continued to eye the room, hoping that his eyes might adjust a little. Then he looked at Ralph, not trying to get free. "Well?"

Ralph looked at him. "I can't, I already tried, before you woke up. Look man, I'm not feeling well."

Donnie slumped back to the gurney. He wiggled things seeing if he could get a strap loose, thinking about what else he could do. "It's probably the drugs."

"I don't think so."

Donnie looked at him. He looked sallow. "What's the matter?"

"I got a real hollow feeling."

Donnie looked down him. "You've probably had a reaction to the drugs," he said. "We'll just get out of here and head to the hospital. It'll be fine."

"I don't feel fine."

"*Help!*" Donnie suddenly screamed. Seemed like a good idea, although he's always the first person to wonder why people who wake up in boxes in films scream for help. It never works. "*Help!*"

"I tried that," Ralph said, weakly.

Donnie stared at him. Face like thunder. "What if there are other customers?" he said, snidely. "Help!" he screamed again. When he stopped, he swallowed. There was a taste of copper, iron maybe, in his throat. "I think I'm getting a cold." There was a petulant moan in his voice.

"That's how mine started. Now I feel sicker."

"Good." Donnie struggled on the gurney again, but his strength depleted quickly. "You reckon we're in the basement."

"It's not my fault."

Donnie shook his head, a noise coming from the darkness. He snapped his head up and looked. "Hello?" he whispered. "Is there someone there?"

A door opened. Shards of light briefly filled the space. The room looking like nothing Donnie had seen before, before being plunged into darkness again. In that glimpse ... the walls red, and wet. A figure slinked in the darkness, before coming close enough for Donnie to see.

The madam.

F I V E

Donnie yanked at whatever bound him. The straps digging deeper into his flesh. He could feel the heat of the cuts as it rose on his skin, welts forming, before he rested back to his gurney. "Bitch," he muttered, just because it made him feel better.

She smiled, coming close enough that he could see her properly.

She didn't look the same as she did in the lobby. Donnie had seen enough videos on the internet to know that makeup could do a job if you knew how to apply it, but it wasn't that. She looked like she was sick. His look tore from her to Ralph. Then back. She looked sick in a different way to Ralph. "What do you want with us?" he snapped, the words spitting from his mouth.

She shook her head. "It's not me you should be asking." Then she laughed. Deep. Hearty. Like she'd just told some fantastical joke in a comedy club.

Donnie just stared at her.

She looked around the darkness, seeing something he couldn't. Before she said, "It won't be long now."

Donnie looked her down. Naked, as she was. Her skin was thin, almost translucent with age. Her tits hung heavy on her chest, but she didn't have the appearance in the face of age. Maybe more of malnutrition. He shook his head. Eyes lingering on what he once coveted. "You need to drink some water," he snapped. He pulled his arms and wrists, turning them gently to try and get them free, pushing, pulling, twisting. His eyes on her, but not looking at her, his mind elsewhere.

She stepped even closer. Her fingers, pale and gaunt, the fingers of a corpse, resting at first down on his shin. From there she slipped them up. Hairs raising in their wake.

Donnie closed his eyes. Damn it. He didn't want that. He didn't want his body to do *that*.

"Oh, yes," she said as his cock rocked lightly to the side. The first sign of arousal.

"Fuck you," he said, looking the other way.

"What the fuck are you doing, man?" shouted Ralph, weakly.

"It's not me," he snarled. His eyes returned to the bitch. "Fuck you," he said, again.

Her smile drew warmth. "Okay," she whispered.

"No." Donnie started to squirm. He looked at Ralph, eyes pleading, but he could see this look in his eyes. Dispair. Pain. Hate.

Fear.

The madam crawled naked on him and started to handle his cock. Her feather touch sparking every hate-filled reaction in his body. Cock hardening. "That's the way," she said. She slipped her head down and took his semi in her mouth. Suckling on it with *expertease*. Head bobbing in rhythm with some unheard music.

Donnie squirmed, "*Fuck off,*" trying to get enough movement in his hips to stop her. To pull it from her.

"I don't feel well."

Donnie looked to Ralph. He didn't look well, either. Getting worse by the second. What the fuck had they done to him? He looked down at the action between his legs, trying to detach himself. Head back. Eyes looking into the darkness over his head.

Then the room filled with a deep grotesque rumble. Sounded like hunger from some impossible stomach. Eyes back on Ralph. His skin was hanging on his face. Didn't look like he had any fat behind it, his skull almost sticking through and out. Donnie raised his head, trying to flick the bitch from him with his hips, but she stayed astride him like she was sucking off a bucking bronco machine.

He came. Didn't mean to. There was no passion behind it as he felt his cum milked from his cock. Drooling slow to her mouth. And when she finally rose from the teat from which she suckled she looked like the woman in the lobby again. An impossible transformation, hag to Goddess. "What the fuck ..." Donnie whispered.

He looked back to Ralph. His skin was slipping from his arms, down by his side, like there was too much of it to cover him now. An ill-fitting skin suit, draped over his skeleton. His ribs visible beyond the arm.

He was being drained of ... everything inside him.

The madam got from Donnie, her body full and beautiful again. Breasts bouncing as she landed back next to him. She wiped the cum from her chin with the back of her hand before licking it off, and swallowing it back. Like her life depended on not wasting a drop. "Thank you," she said. She turned to leave.

"*Tell me,*" Donnie said. "Tell me what's happening."

He could feel the emptiness in his stomach, like a vacuous space needing to be filled, his very being consumed with the want to eat. She came to him. Feeding her cum sticky fingers into his mouth. He hated to lick them, but he did. A hunger, need, so desperate, it overrode rational thought. She watched him, gently stroking her body, feeling the return of the beauty. "It needs to feed just like the rest of us."

Then she slipped her fingers from his mouth and turned, slinking into the darkness. Spittle clung between the tips of her fingers and his lips before dropping away to his skin, leaving him cold, and wet. Dirty. "Jesus …. Fuck," he muttered looking back to Ralph. His skin was pooling, more flexible than loose now, like it was breaking down. Globs of it were started to move to the edge of the gurney, and hang over the side, and the reminiscence of cheese melting from the top of a pizza poorly placed in the oven wasn't lost on him.

"Ralph," he barked. "*Ralph.*"

Ralph turned his head to face him. "It's getting darker in here."

Donnie shook his head. Ralph's irises were a whiter shade of the blue they used to be. Should have been. The pupil's cataracted. Something creamy oozing from the conjunctiva. "You're gonna be fine," he said, turning away. He raised his head and looked down himself. He could see his ribs. That was just the way he was laying, right? He looked at his moobs. They didn't seem any different. Barely noticeable.

The sound of something wet moving caused him to

look to Ralph again. His skin was detaching from his arms, running from the table down to the floor. Ralph's body looked like he was convulsing, but not. "How you feeling?" Donnie asked.

"I don't want to die," Ralph said. He was crying. Blood streaks breaking through the pus almost covering his eyes now, running down into his hair as it was falling from his head. Like he was being digested.

Donnie swallowed back, and could taste blood. Must be from earlier. He could taste blood earlier. The cherries. He remembered the cherries. That was it. They must have drugged him. Maybe that was why it had been so easy to go a second time.

The growling in the room filled the space again, and Ralph cried out. Donnie wasn't able to tell if it was fear or pain. Anguish.

He lay back, unable to get his arms free, and closed his eyes. That was it. The cherries were drugged. Something to make him hard. Knock him out. Now he was down here. It felt like a *down here*. He wiggled his toes. Could still feel them. But it was so cold.

There was another sound. From Ralph. This time is wasn't a scream or a word. It sounded like vomit. He glanced, nothing more. Blood vomiting from Ralph as the room continued to digest him.

Because that was what it was. He closed his eyes again to think. The madam. She'd consumed part of him. It made her whole. That *everything* experience. It was fantasy fulfilment like they could read their minds the whole time.

And now this place was keeping them. He dropped

his head to the side and watched Ralph's skin burn from his ribs. The flesh blackening and drooling from his flesh, little more than a thin layer beneath, then that too, slipping from the bone like a cooked brisket, fourteen hours in the smoker. He was shaking and shuddering. Not dead. Still living through this, *his last experience.*

Donnie closed his eyes, and lay his head back. He doubted anyone was going to come to him again. Not like the madam. His overpowering need was food. He was so hungry. Stomach empty. Fucking cherries. A pain stabbed down his side. Inside. Felt like diverticulitis. Or someone slashing his guts open without breaking the skin. "Shit," he muttered. Heard another movement from next to him and looked. Wished he hadn't. Ralph was little more than poorly digested goo now. Even his bones were looking like they'd been in cola for a week, weird and bendy.

He could taste Ralph in the air. This weird meatiness in breaths. He couldn't breathe through his nose now. Blocked.

Throat felt weirder, too. Like he was having some sort of reaction to something. Closing up. He raised his head again to check out his body, and when he hefted it, it started thumping like he had the worst hangover in the world. That feeling of liquid sloshing around in there. Mouth dry. He blinked his eyes to focus. Hard. Could feel the crusting. That green stuff when you sleep too long.

His stomach growled with dissatisfaction, and the room itself joined in, a chorus of enhungered displeasure. He tried to tell the room to fuck off, but although his mouth and throat were wet and moist, they also felt dry and chaffed. The liquid he swallowed back was bitter and acrid.

A stabbing pain in his back. He cried out. The words to plead with the madam, the room, no longer there. His mind burning with torture. A pain like he'd never felt before rode up his leg, from his foot. Something happened. He tried to lift his head to look, but it was too hard. It felt like something was sticking him to the gurney. His hair stuck to the surface with a strange and unworldly gloop. Quickly, he realised it was his skin. He gripped his hand to a fist, and felt the dermis stretch and split open, burning like he'd just plunged his hand into hot coals. His tears breaking through the sludge that began to bury his eyes as he was digested by the darkness. Blood oozed from the splits in his hand, then followed his arms, and legs. He could feel the skin cracking and breaking. Until it happened on his stomach. The pain was unbearable. His brain detaching, few lucid thoughts still rattling about. Why was this happening? What was it? But the blackness consumed him.

A stab. Popping sound. His left lung collapsing in on itself.

The rupture of pain.

An instinctual movement. He wanted to curl into a ball.

But the binds tore through his flesh as he moved his hands and legs. Feeling the leather of the strap reach the bone, clean through as the flesh was dug out. He pulled his left hand, and the skin, and blood, muscles and tendons were degloved as he pulled, his hand slipping wet and slick through the strap, and out. Free.

An overwhelming sense of *freedom* surrounded him

as he brought his hand up to look at it. Through cataract eye, he saw the sloop of blistered pus that was all that was left of the hand raised. Bones falling away as nothing held them in place any longer.

His thoughts stopping slowly.

A warming lull as the pain stopped.

A blackened hand falling over his eyes.

A serene nothing, as his thoughts calmed and he waited. It was nice with the pain gone from within. He was free of the body. There was no desire. No pleasure. Nothing to be felt from the embrace of the inevitable.

Becoming one with the all consuming.

Peace.

CULT KILLING MONSTERS

There are those people who say that losing your freewill is an abomination, but to those I say, are any of us really free?

"So we're doing this, and Jezza isn't here?"

Yes, we are. And to call the man *Jezza*, I mean, it's a bit rude, isn't it? I've known him for some years now and I'm allowed to call him Jerry, but this fucknut newb should be calling him Jeremy. Like a fucking cuck. I look in the rear-view and shake my head. I flick my lighter open and the flame dances to life, licking up to the roof of the car, the smell of butane reaching my nose. His eyes meet mine and his face morphs to some sadness, like he knows he's said something he shouldn't have. I flick the lighter shut again with a click. Then his stare drops from mine and he continues.

"I just think he should be here himself, is all."

I turn, riding my arm over the passenger seat, so I can look at him without the mirror. He's sitting in the back of the Volvo, next to Johnny. Johnny's a good sort. He's been with us since near the beginning. Back when it was all basement antics and casual beatings. Now it's more serious, and Johnny's not only still with us, but after a slap on the wrist with the local constabulary, he never even thought about giving us up.

That's the sort Johnny is. And that's the sort that gets you promotion. Maybe a lieutenant one day. Won't be today though. That's my job today. Anyhow, I look at the little scrote. I don't know what Jerry sees in him, in all fairness. But that's not my call. What the boss says and all that. We do what he wants without question, and everything turns out in the end. "You know your problem?" I say, jabbing my finger at him to exacerbate the meaning, like. Also, it might be phrased as a question, but it is not a question. "You think the world owes you a favour."

Ray shakes his head. "No way, man."

I glance to Johnny. Dude has his finger up his nose. He's rooting around in there for something. Finds it, apparently. He looks at Ray and then smiles. Then back at me. Then at whatever is stuck to the end of his finger.

"So why the fuck do you think that Jerry should be here?"

"It's his plan, ain't it?" Ray straightens in his seat like he thinks he's got an argument.

"It is, and we are his soldiers, right?" He nods along to this, because he's heard it all before and at this point, disagreeing will end up with something very bad happening. "So when a job needs doing, we do it, right?"

He sighs audibly. "I get it, but—" He stops himself. That or the look on my face did it for him. "I get it," he echoes.

"Good." I turn back in my seat and look out the window. The house that we're targeting is some five doors down. Now most of the time, when you think about people like us taking on a house, you probably think about that Sharon Tate movie, or whatever. Well, it's not really like that. Or, I dunno, maybe it is. I've never seen that shit. Either way. We're in the nicer side of the beachy side of a shit hole town some thirty miles from where we live, sitting in the gutter in a jacked car, waiting for proper dark.

It is dark now, but sort of half-light dark. Makes sense? No? Fine. Anyway. Jerry says we wait until it's dark-dark, and that the Thompson family will put the porch light on at that point. That's when we know to go.

But I don't like sitting here. Not in an area like this. A copper drives by or some old cunt walking his Shih Tzu and we're all made. Not that it would stop us mind, but the chances of us getting away are a whole shit heap smaller.

I don't know. There's some movement in the house we're sitting outside. Curtains closing. I don't trust Ray to do this right. I'd be happier going in with Johnny alone. There's only a couple in there. We can handle that. Them and a kid. Kids are never a problem. Well, depends on the age, but I doubt this will be a problem. The house on the other side of the roads lights go on in the driveway.

Nearly time.

I glance over to Johnny. "You ready?"

"I am," he says, quietly.

"Me too," says Ray.

"I didn't ask." You need to keep these kids in check, am I right?

That's when the porch light goes on at the house we're sitting outside. Fuck this shit. I'm fed up waiting and besides, we're going to get made if we stick out here much longer.

Showtime.

I pull the car along the road a little. Get us a bit closer to the house. We're going to want to get from the house and back to the car pretty sharp, not wandering about like sight-seers. In case someone sees us, right? We might be a mess. So, I crawl it along, in the curb. The car's a piece of shit, but it starts nice and reliably. Which is also something of a plus. Can you imagine it? Sitting there covered in bits of Thompson and the car's like, *hur-hur-hur-click*. Man. I wouldn't want to be in those shoes. Ha. So, anyway, lights off, I crawl to the edge of the drive, but not across. Don't want to raise suspicion with the neighbours, now, do I? Then I kill the engine. Wait a second. Then we're out.

Two adults. One kid. Shouldn't be a problem. Don't know how old the kid is. I can always hope for a baby. Babies are the easiest, big time. I glance to Ray as I push myself from the driver's seat. Him and Johnny are getting out the back. It's go time, so we're silent. At least the kid knows that much. But I don't trust him enough to give him a part of the job to himself. Not even a baby. He might fuck it up, see?

On the driveway.

I point down the side of the house, and head in that direction. Johnny will take the front door. He'll give me a minute to get around the back. Ray's coming with me. I go down the sideway. A light comes on, motion sensor. I don't look up at it. It is the worst thing you can do. If there's a camera up there, you've looked straight into it. Ray probably looked into it. But that's not my problem. Jerry can deal with that later. Castrate him or cut off his head. Either way. Like I said. Not my problem. Also—look casual. If you look casual, most people ignore you.

Look like you're meant to be there.

What am I telling you for, anyway? You're just here for the jollies, am I right? Anyhow, me and Ray continue around the back. Thing with rich people, is that they tend not to have the security of the poor. You try getting into the back garden of someone living on a housing estate. Fucking dogs, and gates, and ... this one house right, I found a fucking bear trap in the middle of the lawn. I shit you not. Can't afford fags, buys a bear trap. I mean where the fuck do you get a bear trap in England? Okay, probably Amazon, but still. I'll check later. Let you know.

Round into the garden. Not even a gate. Probably no camera. I'll ask Ray if he saw one when he was gawping at the light, later.

Nice garden. Got gnomes. Long patio doors. Probably bi-fold. Fancy. Window in the kitchen. I look quickly through the kitchen window. I can't see a light in there, but I'm careful just in case some cunt is standing there doing the dishes in the dark.

But it looks empty.

Then I wave Ray forward. I assume he's still behind me, and it might behove me to check, but I don't because I don't have time. Along the rest of the wall to the doors. There is a light illuminating the patio, coming from inside. I can see a flicker of something moving. Could be the TV. But that means they're inside there.

I stop, and look around the door. Fuck a duck this place is nice. These people aren't just outwardly rich. They're clearly rich-rich. I stay right to the side of the door, so as not be seen by anyone glancing in the vague direction of the garden, casually. Which isn't a problem, because they're all busy in there.

I rock back, lean my back against the wall, Ray

standing there behind me, looking a little impatient, and also a little nervous. "Well?" he says. "We going?"

"One second." I need to mentally prepare. I'm going to try the bi-folds first, and if they're locked we're going to have to storm the house. Been there and done that, so no problems from that point. However, there is more than just the couple and kid. There's someone else in there on the sofa. I glance to Ray. "You ready for this?"

"I'm ready," he replies.

He's not ready. Christ. I'm not ready. Not having just seen *that*. I reach over and grip the latch on the door and squeeze. Motherfucker is unlocked. We're straight in. I push the door open, just a little. Enough to make it easy to push wide.

There's a muffled scream.

Ray goes to move, he panics. We've been made.

But I stop him. Shake my head before he rushes in there and fucks everything up. Raise my finger for him to wait. He looks pissed, but intrigued. He might be growing on me. Cocky little bastard. Another muffled cry. I can feel him tense. But he doesn't move this time.

Then I push the door open, slowly, with one hand, pulling the knife I brought with me out with the other. It's a nice knife. Came out of the shed back at the farm.

I step in. Ray follows. He breathes in, air catching in his lungs.

He wasn't expecting this either.

See, Mr. Thompson is naked, as is Mrs. Thompson, and the interloper, the third party, is also naked. The interloper, is on the sofa, facing a roaring open fire, and each of the Thompson's are on either side of her. Each of them going to town. Hands and fingers everywhere. Tongues too. But no one is paying attention to me and Ray. Ray has a grin on his face like he's just walked onto a porn set, which I suppose I can understand.

That's when Johnny wanders into the living room from the other side of the house. I look to him, eyebrows up, like how the fuck…?

He shrugs and says, "The front door was open." He bites into the apple he got from somewhere. I have to remember to ask where he got that from.

Oh yeah. And that was when they noticed three blokes standing there watching them fuck. The weird thing was, was that they didn't seem all that bothered. I don't know what I would have done, you know, if I was railing one of my wives and I look up to find some dude standing there eating an apple watching, but I like to think I would have done *something*.

This dude, Mr. Thompson, he looks at me. Sort of half rocks over to his side and 'points' at me with his … you know … thing. Got this girl half underneath him. Mrs. Thompson just lays there. She's frozen in time. Looks like a ren painting. You know the ones with the lounging naked chicks. Girl in the middle only looks about … I'm no good at this shit. She's a teenager, maybe. The babysitter? It's always the babysitter in these things, isn't it? A shit ton younger than Mr. and Mrs. T, anyway. Mr. T. frowns at me. He looks rightfully annoyed, but doesn't do the usual. He doesn't explode or anything. He just sort of stares at me for a moment. His willy bounces up and down like he's excited, which is weird.

Actually, this is all pretty weird.

"Can I help you?" he asks.

Very British. He's probably good at queuing, too. Mrs. T. then moves herself from her elbow, mouth hovering over their third-party's tit, and she looks at me. She looks me down. Raises one appraising eyebrow, and then looks at Ray. Shakes her head and returns her look to me. A fine looking woman, for sure, but we're not here for that.

The babysitter is still heaving air in and out of her lungs like she was really close to finishing herself up when we intervened. Shame. Especially now she's collateral.

"Jeremy sent us."

Mr. T. frowns a big one. "Cock," he mutters under his breath. He starts to get up, pushing himself off the poor young woman who was taking so much of his weight, and I step forward. Knife goes up a bit. I'll be honest, I like this sort of gig. It sits well with me, but as I'm being honest, I'd rather draw it out a little than just finish it here and now, you know? Enjoy the process. Everyone should like their job and Jerry will treat me good for this one. Mr. T. gets the picture and slumps back down on the sofa. Off the girl. His cock is still raging hard. Which is good for him, I guess. Man of his declining years being able to pop a stiffy so hard he can't get rid of it even with extra blokes in the room. Unless that's his jam, of course. I shudder. My eyes go to Johnny, still eating his apple. "Go and find the kid," I say.

Johnny nods.

Mr. T. says, "There isn't anyone else here."

I nod, to tell him I heard him, but I'm fine with Johnny going and finding the kid anyway. "So," I ask, "You have to pop a blue pill to hit a chubby that hard?"

His look doesn't waver from me when he smiles, but I hear Mrs. T. snort out a laugh. Then his eyes jerk down to his erection and he grabs it. Pulls the skin up the side like he's about to start jerking off, a bulge of pre-cum bulbs at the top and he releases it.

Fucking weirdo.

"No," he replies. "Definitely not." He smiles at me wider. Like there's a joke there I don't know. I hear Johnny thumping around upstairs. A quick glance to the ceiling. Then back to the terrible threesome. The girl in the middle has calmed down a bit and now she has her forefinger in her mouth, like she's enjoying all this, and I'm pretty sure she's eye-fucking me. Not that I'm any good on picking up any of those sorts of signals. Well, to be honest, I've been with Jerry so long now, I don't need to pick up on anything like that anymore. It all gets sort of handed to me.

I circle the room slowly, getting myself behind the sofa with my back to what looks like the door into the kitchen. That way they can't see me, she's got to stop eye-fucking me, and I don't need to look at that guys dong anymore. But I motion for Ray to stay where he is. Covering the exits, if you get me. Also, it means he has to look at that guy's dong, and that makes me warm inside. I smile to myself, watching him try to look hard with his knife, all the while trying not to look at the dude's cock. He also seems to be averting his eyes from the chicks too. I wonder if Jerry has something to do with that. Some promise of a virgin if he behaves.

Wouldn't be the first time Jerry has made that sort of promise.

Johnny makes too much noise coming back down the stairs, and into the living room through the door to the hallway. I glance back. Prick doesn't have the kid. "The fuck?" I ask him. He shrugs.

"There ain't no one here." He gestures down to the threesome. "Just them."

"I told you," Mr. T. interrupts.

Now I'm not one to lose my temper easily, but I have to restrain myself from clubbing him with the hilt of my knife just for his insolence. Wanker.

"Where is it?" I hiss.

Mr. T. turns on the sofa, arching himself over the back of it. "I told you there wasn't anyone else here," he says. "Just us." He waves his hands in front of the women. I can't see him, but I think in the middle of the gesture he squeezes the babysitters tit, because not only does he linger, his look darts over there, the babysitter sucks air in through gritted teeth, and Ray shakes his head and respectfully looks the other way.

"There isn't a kid's room up there," Johnny responds. "Not a kid-kid." He stares at me firm. Trying to tell me something. His eyes burn into mine. Darting to the threesome. Back to me. Back at them. I follow his glare.

To the babysitter.

I round, back to where I came from. "Mr. Thompson," I start. I can see Ray looking at me, wondering what's going on. "Is this your daughter?" I ask. The words falter slightly in my mouth, because, well, you know, I just can't quite believe I'm saying them.

Mr. T. looks at the girl in the middle. *The babysitter.* And then across her to the wife. He tenderly brushes his hand down the girl's chest, before returning his eyes to me. A small smile. "Of course," he says.

Ray makes this sound like shit being stamped down like a waffle into the plug of a running shower. Don't ask me how I know what that sounds like. Johnny looks nonplussed. I myself must have had some sort of look on my face, because Mr. T. chuckles at me.

"My boy," he says, "who did you think it was?"

"Anyone else," I reply, without thinking.

He shakes his head.

Then I hear something else. I'm not the only one, either. It's coming from the hallway. Shit. Johnny is already on the turn heading back to the door, partially closed behind him. He's got his knife up, and I know from past experience he can take care of whatever is out there.

"You *were* early," Mr. T. says.

I look to them, then to Ray. He's white as a fucking sheet. Damned kids. Shouldn't be involved in a job like this. I *knew* he wasn't ready. Then I edge towards the door. Halfway around the sofa. I'm losing control of the room. I've got a kid on crowd control. Johnny's now running security on his own. I'm kinda lost. "What the fuck do you mean?" I hiss at the fucker. "Early?"

Then there are voices. Johnny pulls the door open, and I can see the shadows for myself. There are a lot of fucking people out there all of a sudden. This shit's gone to the dogs. What are we, in the wrong house? Johnny just stands there. He's better than that, so I don't know what to make of it, for a moment. He backs away. Turns. His eyes meet mine, and they're saying one thing.

Abort.

I glance to Ray. I have to make that split second decision. But it's too late to. The house appears to be filling up with bodies. Too late, either way. Johnny's back, passing the sofa and heading towards the patio doors. He's legging it, without say so. Okay. I'll cut his balls off for that later. But I'm no longer on the fence about fucking off. I gesture for Ray to follow, before giving Mr. T., Mrs. T., and the T. kid, a last glance. "Freaks," I mutter, turning to follow the others out the house.

But Johnny is at the door and the door isn't moving.

"You didn't think I was going to let you scurry back off home, did you?" says Mr. T. I turn back and look at him. He's pushing himself from the sofa. Standing. He *still* has that massive great boner. "Like rats," he says. There is something far more sinister in the back of his voice now.

It scares me.

I hold my knife out at him. Like a gangster with a gun. "Back the fuck up," I bark. I don't look, but my next words are to Johnny. "What the fuck's happening? Open the Goddamned door."

"I can't man, it's locked or jammed or something."

"Here," says Ray.

I hear him pushing Johnny out the way. The kid's scared, which I sort of get, but he can't lose it. Not right now.

Then the door to the living room opens and people start to come in. They're all dressed in fucking dinner jackets and shit. It looks like the march of the fucking penguins.

Like, what the fuck?

"Hello, Charles," says Mr. T., rounding the sofa, hand out to shake. Like it's all completely natural. Three dudes with knives. Fucking the daughter on the sofa. I back away, towards Johnny. Charles, apparently, then looks at me.

"They're early," he says.

This is about where I get that sinking feeling. You know the one. For you, it might be when you're on your way to see your kids flute recital, or drop a cheque in the bank. The roads are blocked. A pile up on the M25 (like always) or it starts fucking snowing and the grandma in the Ford Ka in front of you wants to do four miles per hour and you are absolutely knackered. You know. When you're in the kitchen naked, waiting to surprise your other half with something special for dinner and when the door goes you suddenly remember that they are bringing your niece and nephew home with them and now you're trapped. Naked and afraid.

That feeling, you know?

Like you're well and truly fucked.

That was the feeling I got just then.

Ray is rattling the door harder than if he was shaking a baby to make it stop crying. Johnny looks pissed, to be honest, but he's not giving a lot away. That just leaves me. My piss has disappeared back up into my body. I don't know what to do. The people keep coming. Apparently Mr. T. was expecting quite the audience for his little incest party. I realise that I'm going to have to start hacking. That's a lot of bodies, but as Ray and Johnny appear to be incapable of getting the door open, I reckon the front door is the future.

So I step in and stab Mr. T. It seems fairly reasonable as it was what Jerry sent us in to do, after all. Get in. Kill the family. Get out.

The knife slides in with ease, as I expected. I've done this once or twice before as you might have expected by this point. The steel slips in to the hilt and I can feel the warmth of his flesh on mine, my hand touching his belly fat. Our eyes meeting. He looks … unsurprised. It's about the best description I can think of for it. He looks like he has present face. You know, when you get socks for Christmas and you have to look like, *great, this is the best*. Sorry. I'm rambling. I pull the knife out and he staggers.

Still has a hard-on, mind, but I'm not getting into that.

He stumbles back into Charles' arms. "Oh," he says. Mr. T., not Charles. "My."

I was hoping that this was going to spur Ray and

Johnny into action, but it hasn't. They're gawping now like they've never seen a man knifed before, although, granted, a great deal of this interaction is crossing new ground.

Charles sticks his fingers in Mr. T.'s wound. Two of them. Like finger guns. He slips the barrel in, and withdraws it. The man's blood slicked over his fingers like he's stuck them in a pot of jam. He raises it up and the attending crowd—there must be six or seven of them in the room by now—all seem to make noises of glee.

Then he stuffs them in his mouth. Eating the blood from his fingers. Felating his finger guns like he's about to blow his own head off.

Then Charles pushes Mr. T. back to his feet, allowing his to take his own weight. "Well," Mr. T., says. "You do have some fight in you, don't you?"

So fuck this shit.

I jam the knife into him again. A little higher on the torso, somewhere up nearer the lungs and heart. Knife goes in, knife comes out.

When I pull the blade this time, I do it with a little more flourish and this dude's blood and goo spits out around the room like I'm flicking paint for a modern art exhibit. Mr. T. staggers, but I'm no longer interested. I turn on my heels, hoping the Johnny and Ray are going to do something of some use. I turn on the wife and daughter of this weird little fam. The wife is up. She's laughing like this is some joke or a fucking street play. One of those dinner time murder mystery parties with added incest. I slash the blade across her. I know it's sharp because it's mine. The steel slips into her flesh without issue, this cut running from the top of her left tit, down, across, all the way to her right thigh. She lurches back a little, then looks down before the wound opens. It's fucking deep. Where it's on her gut it, opens up like the grand canyon and I can see her fucking guts pushing to free themselves like sausages in an over filled carrier bag. We've all done that right? The bag splitting in the street. Sausages falling asunder.

No? That just me?

Anyway. I raise my foot up and kick her, hard. Right in the bulging intestines and she tumbles backward, falling into the open fire.

The daughter barely glances at her. She comes at me. At least the little one has some fight. A quick glance down her, and the thought crosses my perverted little mind that it's going to be a shame to fuck up her body, but I guess now isn't the time for a recruitment drive, and I guess I have to kill her.

Those were the orders after all.

I spin the knife, all cool like, and twist it to back hand, bringing my hand up like Michael fucking Myers, and stab down onto her. I don't really care where I hit her, because this knife is nearly as big as she is, and wherever it is, it's probably going to kill her. At least I'm saving her money on years of therapy, right?

As it happens, she makes a weird flail and the knife jams down directly into her skull. She goes all sorts of limp and stiff, kinda at the same time, and when I pull the knife out, she drops. Gives me a chance to look at Mrs. T., who has rolled from the fire, blood gushing hard and fast from her guts and tit, and such, but her flesh, in the fire, has boiled and blistered, popped. The pus running out into her blood, flesh sticking to the wood, the burning hot fireplace, skin torn from her body.

It's enough to make you feel … something.

I look over. Johnny and Ray *have* taken my lead. Johnny is doing a sterling job of getting violent with the suits, evening dresses, that sort of thing. Ray as taken one of them in particular down. An older gentleman, by the look of it. Hard to tell at the moment, to be sure. He's got the guy on the floor and straddled him, and the knife is going up and down like a jackhammer. He must have stabbed the guy four times in the time I've watched him, maybe five seconds.

Wow.

He's really going postal.

But he is slowing. Probably tired.

I step over Charles. His throat is a gash of goo. Gash of goo. I like that. Johnny's cut him open, and he's pissing blood. I'm surprised, actually, there seems to be more blood in him than I thought possible. He's still breathing mind. I can see his eyes, watching me. Hand up on his throat like he's trying to stem the flow or some shit. It doesn't work like that. You have about ninety seconds to stop the bleeding or you die. And he's got too much blood loss for it to have been less than that.

My shoes make a squelching sound when it sinks into the blood sodden shag. The white carpet, red. Fuck. I was hoping not to have to need to wash those. Fucks up trainers putting them in the washing machine. I know, I know. Even in a pillow case to stop them rattling around too much.

Johnny jams his blade into some bitches shoulder. She grunts. He pulls it out, and she doesn't drop, which is a surprise. Johnny then grabs the front of her dress and yanks it, down hard. Pulls it open. Gets to see her body. Same as me. She's hot, yes. But not what we're here for, and Johnny knows that. But you have to let him have his fun.

Instead of screaming though, she looks like she's into it. Makes a sound more like she's about to come than she's just been stabbed. It certainly throws Johnny off his game, so he steps up to the plate, and grabs her hair with one hand, dragging her head back, and with the other, he stabs his knife into her throat. Her eyes wide. She grins. Blood starts to drool from her mouth before anything else, and when Johnny pulls the blade, the broken artery spouts one single spurt, flying across the room, then blood gushes out of her like Niagara Falls. She chokes out some blood, the lot of it slipping down her face, off, onto her naked body. Ray's stopped. The man (ex-man) beneath him having had a tirade of a hundred or more stab wounds, is now a jumbled mess of meat and bone. Flesh in flaps hanging off, while things that should be on the inside have hacked off bits on the outside. Ray himself is heaving air in and out of his lungs. Little dude is out of shape. I'll have to talk to him later. He's done a cracking job on that dude, but me and Johnny have taken responsibility for more than our fair share of the work.

I step over an eyeball that appears to have loosed from one of the bodies.

They're all down now. Apart from Mr. T. He's still on his feet. Leaning back against the sofa. He's awfully white, though. Lost a lot of blood. It's all down his body, painting him red like fucking war paint or some shit.

"Right," I say. I step over Charles. Blood still oozing from his wounds.

"Right," says Mr. T., groggily.

I raise my blade up, pushing it to that bit of flesh under the chin. The soft bit where I can push it through into his mouth with ease. Something still bothers me. "Why did you say we were early?" I ask him.

He simply draws a smile, and replies, "Because you were."

I don't have time for this shit. So I push the blade up into his head. It goes through the mouth, cutting the front of the tongue off, through the plate on the top of the mouth and into the brain. I assume. I don't really know how far around the inside of the head the brain goes. Either way, when I pull the blade out, there's this weird yellow substance on the end of it, and Mr. T.'s right eye falls slightly to about four o'clock, all the while the other still stares at me. So I guess, yes, I did hit the brain. He won't go down, so I push him over the back of the sofa, and he rolls over, blood smearing the leather.

I look quickly around, and take in a deep breath. The place smells like a butchery. Not a good one either. The scent of coppers and irons hanging heavy in the room filled with a wet moisture in the air. It's thick. Warm. I look down to Ray still heaving air into his lungs and staring at the meaty corpse on the ground beneath him. He suddenly seems to realise that he's there, or the meatbag is there or something, because he pushes himself up from the corpse.

I look a little closer.

Nope. Dude is still breathing. Um. Yay? Christ, it must smart. He's still aware. He's still looking between us, his fleshy bits still moving up and down.

"Right," I say, glancing back around. "Jerry isn't going to be pleased about that." There's a wheezing sound from behind the sofa. Then a lulled quiet. Maybe Mr. T. finally died? "Let's go," I tell the two of them, passing both of them, into the hallway.

"Are we just leaving?" says Ray. There's a shake in his voice, like he might have shit himself.

"We are." I wave my bloody knife back, gesturing to the corpse pile. "Ain't none of them getting back up. We'll let them bleed out quietly." My hand hits the door handle. But it won't budge. "Fuck," I hiss. They fucking locked the door on the way in. I don't rattle it like in they do in films. That's show, don't tell. I don't need to do that, because that's not how door handles work. "Right," I say. I'm buying time, deciding what to do for the best. "Let's just get out a window."

Then I turn back, facing Ray and Johnny behind me. And behind them is fucking Mr. Thompson. He's standing in the doorway, covered in fucking blood. I thought I'd killed his brain to be honest, but apparently not. Huh. He also still has an erection, which is weird for many reasons now, not least of which is that he probably shouldn't have that much blood left in his torso to … you know … maintain that sort of malarkey.

He raises his hand while I'm staring at him, and points. Then I remember that I cut his tongue off and he probably can't say a lot. So I say it for him. "Cunt." It was probably what he was thinking.

That spurs Johnny and Ray to turn and look at him, and I step between them. Better end this now. Knife up. Except Mr. T. doesn't move much, his hand is still pointing, and it crosses my mind that maybe he is mostly brain dead and that he's moving only on instinct. I step in, back to my Myers impression but before I plunge the knife in (I was going to go all Ray on him this time, and see how many times I could stab him before my anger and bitterness of this situation drained from me) he lurches with some inhuman speed to the side and his pointing hand becomes his slapping hand and I'm up in the air and bouncing off the wall like I'm being tossed around by a pro-wrestler.

I crash down. Apparently I don't bounce well, because everything suddenly hurts, and all I can hear is this high pitched whine in my ears like I was too close to the amp stack at a Pantera concert last night. Johnny and Ray have my back though and they bundle in on the cunt. I don't know. Must have hit my head because it doesn't look like it's going so well for them. Like Mr. T. has too many arms and he's everywhere.

I blink away the tiredness in my eyes. Can't afford to take a nap about now. I feel around. Knife's gotta be there somewhere. My hand, flat on the floor, I push to get myself up to sitting.

There's a spiking pain moving up my arm and by Christ, it hurts. Must have twisted something. Then Johnny hits the floor. Over by the front door. He slumps, sliding down the door to the floor. A spap of blood there, on the white of the double-glazed door. Banged his head or some shit.

Ray shouts, "Fuckers," and starts slashing his blade about and wailing on Mr. T.

Maybe I misjudged him? He might be a good lad. I twist my body around a little, but I might have ruptured something.

You know what? I think I might need to take a quick rest.

Fuck it. I'm still on the floor. Unmoved. At least the fucking police haven't dragged me down the cells. I guess Ray did his job. Shit. I hope Johnny's okay. I can smell death. Good. Those fuckers will have been diced up like beef. At least, the way I saw Ray going at it. I can hear dripping. Little sploots of wet. *Blip. Blip. Blip.* There's a slight sweet smell in the air, too. And it's hot. Like sticky. I can feel it on my skin.

The room's hazy when I open my eyes. Must have hit my head real fucking hard. Bastard will have gotten what's coming to him, though. Fucker must have worked out. Damn. I can't see so much as feel this weird funk around me. There's a sort of bubble gum pink hue to everything, and as my vision starts to clear, I see movement on the other side of the room.

I blink it out. Try to move. What the fuck is going on? I … I can't move. Not properly anyway. I jerk my head up. A little panic there, that's for sure. The thump of pain from a head blow stabs at the back of my skull and my eyes feel heavy. On the other side of the room is Johnny. He's laying on the floor. Body's twisted a little. Legs going out one way and arms the other.

The whoosh of blood in my ears clears and I can hear him screaming. Not in pain. But in fear.

"Johnny," I shout back. "Johnny man, what the fuck's going on?" I pull at my arms, my legs. Nothing moves. Wild, I look down myself. I've been covered in this ... shit. It looks like deep pink goo, hardened, like fucking builder's foam or some shit. It strings from the floor over me, and it's hard as fucking nails. I kick at it with what little movement I have in my feet, but there's nothing. Squirming and wriggling, I can't get free.

Johnny screams again, drawing my attention back to him. He shouts, "Help me, fucking ... help me."

He's on the floor. This gunk shit is on his hands. Now I know what it is, I can see it holding him down. In fact, it's fucking everywhere. It looks like a P.E. sufferer has just had an accident in a sex shop. But pinker, you get me? Whatever. Attention back to Johnny. His feet are at the door to the living room and that's where his attention appears to be. Then a hand comes from the room. Down on the floor. Like someone's at his feet. It grabs his foot. It's raw. Like whoever's hand it is has been scratching too much. Glowing, almost, with this inhuman heat. Then the other hand, and they crawl up him, hand over hand like he's a fucking gym rope. His screams become indecipherable. He stops squirming. I can see the dark patch bloom on the front of his clothes. Oh, Johnny, man. You're better than that. We'll get out of this.

Whatever *this* is.

The hands continue up him, as it appears, Mr. Thompson, is pulling himself up Johnny's torso. Damn. I wasn't expecting him to still be in the land of the living, to be honest. "Ray," I shout. "Where the fuck are you?"

Mr. T. gives me a look. A quick one. His eyes say I'm next. He's hungry looking. Skin on his face like that of his hands, and arms, seeing more of his flayed body as he pulls himself through the doorway.

Until I see his hips. He's ... no. This doesn't make sense. Maybe I banged my head too hard? From the waist down, he doesn't have normal ... bits? What the fuck am I even saying? He drags his torso through, and there are no hips, no legs, he's like a fucking snake from there down. Fucking damp, pink, sticky snake. I realise I've stopped screaming for Ray. I'm just fucking mouth breathing. Hard. My heart hammers in my chest and I seem to have lost feeling in my fingers.

Christ. Gotta pull myself together.

Johnny's not screaming anymore, either. He's just watching this ... *fucking thing* ... pull itself up him, a fucking snake-man. Thing. Johnny's eyes are wide. He's not breathing. Holding it. I can see it. His face, white as a fucking sheet. Then, Mr. T. rolls to his side, revealing his belly to Johnny. That's when Johnny starts screaming again. From around where his belly button should be there's this weird snake like proboscis sticking from him. Looks like a pig's snout on the end. A couple of holes, and snot drooling from it. It extends in size, coming from the belly of the creature. I'm not even gonna equate it to the man we were sent here to fucking kill. It's just a thing now. The snout turns, like it has a mind of its own and studies Johnny.

Johnny whispers, "No," staring back into the thing like its got eyes. Like he can see inside the things soul.

There's pain in my feet, and I suddenly realise that I'm kicking this shit that's holding me down. Over and over, as hard as my muscles can.

The proboscis snakes its way over Johnny, the same shit holding him down, and the weight of this creature on his legs. The hands, they start to claw at Johnny's clothes, tearing at them, frantic, like a lover, desperate to get to the flesh beneath, pulling his shirt open. Then the thing snakes to him. Snout down. It seems to sniff at him a couple of times. Then it touches him. Johnny stops moving. I can see it in his eyes though. It's not that the thing has done shit all to him. He's just frozen in fear.

Same as me. I can feel tears stinging my eyes. Where the fuck is Ray?

The snout moves and Johnny screams again. This time it *is* pain. The snot on it, it fucking burns his skin away like piss on toilet paper.

I'm kicking harder. My foot's hot. Pretty sure I'm bleeding in my shoe. Still. Better that, than … *that*.

The snout charms its way, snaking into his burnt open flesh, its acidic goo opening Johnny up like an over ripe banana. The thing pushes its way in, burning an opening. He screams, cutting the air. It's the worst thing I think I ever heard. Jesus wept. The snout, it enters him, sliding in, raping his torso. It's pushing shit about in there. I can see the bulges and lumps appear as the thing attached to the monster moves his innards about. It's pushing up his body.

Johnny stops screaming. He's rocked his head back. Looking the other way. His eyes are wide, but while his life is still there, there's no soul. His mouth hangs open. I can see the proboscis slithering around inside him, burning his guts away, stopping him from breathing. He twitches. His life pushing out of him in one last effort, then his throat bulges as the thing pushes up, up. His face burns a fleshy red and then melts away, the creature's sex thing fucks a hole into his face. Out. The snout looking now at me.

"Sooooo … gooooooooood," the creature wheezes from Thompson's mouth.

I look down. My foot has penetrated this shit holding me down and continues to break it away, chipping at it. My leg is torn to ribbons, blood slicking out of my shins where I keep kicking without thought.

The snake slips back into Johnny's corpse and winds its way back to the entrance. The acid still burning away at him, turning Johnny's skin into ash, the flesh melting down to the floor like something out of an eighties horror flick. Globules of flesh balling up and hanging like rolled snot, dripping to the floor and staining the carpet.

Then it's out. Free. It's looking at me. I don't know how, or why, but I know that the snout of the creature is *looking* at me.

My knee is free. I can move my arm a little. Get some leverage on my body to move it.

But my heart sinks when something else—someone else—crawls through the door. It's the daughter. What's left of her anyway.

"Consume …" she seems to say, the word creeping from her mouth, as she drags her legless body forward.

I don't think this is good news, to be honest.

She's gouged open in the middle of her head, from where I'd shanked her. And as she comes around the door, I see she is without proboscis. Instead rocking a massive looking vagina slit.

"Consume ... ate." *Consummate.* She pulls herself up Thompson, and the proboscis's attention is taken from me. To her. Then she slides up her father, his human hands, pulling at her breasts, their skin as red as each other's. The proboscis rolls around itself trying to find her entrance, before it slides into her. The girl creature hisses air in, braying her head back as the Thompson creature buries his face in her chest. His proboscis pulls quickly from her body as fluids gush from the snout, covering the lower half of the both of them. He raises his head from her and cries out. Somewhere lost between pleasure and pain.

I think I just saw this fucking thing prematurely ejaculate inside its own daughter monster. Not that it seems to matter, nor put it off.

The Thompson head bows back down to the daughter's breasts, taking them in its mouth, raw as they are, covering them in lesions and welts as it bites and pulls, it's snout shaking its ejaculate from itself, and then plunging back into the daughters gape.

It appears they prefer to have sex after eating instead of the other way around. I myself like a pizza, after being balls deep in one of my wives. You?

Frozen by the show, I suddenly push myself back into action, and raise my knee with such force I break open the shitty pink prison and find myself able to push and pull myself out of it. A quick glance to Thompson and he appears to be going at the girl like a jack hammer, and far less concerned with me. The two of them slipping desperately around in the ejaculate, it lubing their whole athletic concerto.

I roll off to the side. Heaving air into my lungs. Exhausted. My legs fucking hurt. I don't think I've broken anything bone-wise, but there's blood leeching into the fabric of my trousers, mixing with all the other fluids I appear to have gained on myself.

A hand clamps on to the doorframe. Shit. I roll up onto my arse and scoot across the floor. I've gotta get out of here. Fuck Ray. I glance to Johnny's corpse his face is now a melted mess of shit. Then up, to the door behind him. That one was locked. So was the back.

No. This is no good at all. I look, frantically, around the room, looking for an exit. The stairs. I can go upstairs. The thing that was about to come around the doorframe manages it. I thought it was going to be the wife, but worse, I think, it's Charles. Balls. He probably wants to probe me. Fucking hell.

I push myself shakily to my feet. I have weird globs of something all over me. My trousers are torn, and I think I might have been sick on myself at some point, none of which is particularly pertinent, but worth mentioning if this is ... *the end* ... so to speak. Charles stops and seems to spend a second looking at Mr. T. and Baby T. fucking, and then his—its—attention returns to me.

I flounder a little to get my legs doing what I require of them. See, I want to be climbing the stairs, and they don't. The pain splinters through me as I step forward, I think, from the prison breaking kicking antics, and I nearly lose my footing entirely. The room swirls as my head spins, and I think I'm going to puke. I know that if I stop, or worse, black out, then I'm fucked. Which in this situation is far worse than the usual sort of 'fucked' I get myself into. I push through the pain and bound (hobble) towards the stairs, pushing my foot flat down on Charles' slug-butt. He hisses out some abandon and twists to get his hands to me, but I'm lucking it out and prove a little too nimble. Crashing over the two fucking and to the floor, I evade Charles' grasp and drag myself to the stairs, pulling myself up. Burning hot agony, as my nails rip free from my fingers as I claw the carpet dragging my torso up, looking, I'm sure just like one of them. These fucking ... things.

Getting my feet back under me. A glance to Mr. T. and he looks to be totally taken by the throes of passion, them taking over, and Charles is still slithering toward me. Johnny's just a blob now. Mostly what's left of him appears to be in the air, as fumes. He fucking stinks, too. Behind Charles is the door back into the living room, and beyond that it looks like there is a whole orgy going on. I can see Ray in there. He's being held by two of the males while two of the females are pulling him apart. The males have his hands, arms, that sort of thing, he's naked, and the females are clawing at his arsehole. Pulling it open.

He's not screaming and I can't see his face, so I don't know if he's dead, unconscious, or has the pain tolerance of a woman. But they crack him open like an Easter egg on Sunday morning, his skin splitting to a gape and the room floods with the stink of his bowels, spilling out to the floor. I see the shit, before I smell it. They're scooping it out, like food fiends at a chocolate fountain, and shovelling it into their gullets like they might starve. His guts, innards, all sorts are coming out too, as they hollow him out anus end first, blood dribbling and drooling to the floor beneath, mixing in with everything else the rather disgusting eaters had left to fall to the side.

Charles reaches the bottom of the stairs, hand over hand, drawing himself closer. I back the fuck up. I just need to get out of here—now. At the top of the stairs, I find the wherewithal to turn around and get from my arse, reverse scooching, and get back to my oh-so wobbly feet. Crashing through the first door I stumble into the bathroom. Big family affair. Nice. I yank the blinds down from the lintel, not concerned with opening them, and the window is a fuck off great fixed pane with a top hung over it, probably about big enough to get a cat through. Maybe Ray on a thin day. I turn back to the door and slam it shut. There's no fucking lock. What kind of bathroom doesn't have a lock on the Goddamn door? I remember the party the fam were engaged in when I broke in and I suppose that answers that. Scratching on the door. Charles is out there, probably trying to pull himself around to an angle that will give him access to the doorknob. What the fuck are those things? What the fuck is going on? I shake the thoughts from my head. I don't have time to worry about that now.

The door handle turns. I'm just staring at it. Paralysed. Shit. I slam my shoulder to the door just as it starts to open and stop it. But I can't close it. The fucking thing is strong, and girthy. Christ. It's pushing it open, and I can't fucking stop it.

I jam my feet firm on the carpet—what kind of monster has carpet in the bathroom?—and then the carpet starts to move. Pushing across the floor, out from under the door. Fuck. I look around the room. Holding the progress of this thing as much as I can. Its proboscis creeps around the door snuffling around, trying to find me. I move my feet to stay out of its way, but that allows movement on the door, a little further open.

I release the door and lurch to the bath, grab the shower rail and yank it hard from the walls. It was suckered up one end—the other I pull the screws from the wall. Spin the thing around like Jackie-fucking-Chan and face this monster down. Charles, there, the door open. His snout is facing me, winding like a snake, like he has no control over it. Must be his cock, then, I guess. "What the fuck are you?" I scream into its face.

The sound of an orchestra's worth of orgasms are rising from the floor below.

Gross.

Charles reaches his hand out, passing the proboscis, his skin bulging and broken, the skin burning with redness, lesions, lacerations on the surface as the under-flesh grows and warps almost making it unrecognisable. "Want," the thing hisses.

Want.

You can want all you fucking like, motherfucker. I jump forward, the curtain rod out in front of me like a spear and I jab the cunt in the face. The skin tears easy. Easier than I thought, but it's tight. Like a balloon. It pops as it tears and the things under-flesh pushes out, like a fat guy in an ill fitting suit bursting open. The room fills with the rancid stench of rotting guts, mixed with something popcorny. Fairground. That's what it reminds me of. I pull back the rod and jam it into the creatures face again. I'm not trying to kill it or anything. In truth I don't know what I'm trying to do. I just want to fucking leave. The second jabbing tears more of the creatures face and it howls out in pain this time—as if I didn't hurt it the first time. It rocks on its side like a beached whale, and I rush past. Its tentacle grabs at me, wet snout sliding about, but I avoid it like the plague, remembering what its goo did to Johnny. Out to the hall. There are more of them. On the stairs. Following the sound, after the conclusion of their fuckfest downstairs, apparently I'm pudding.

Fuck that. I swing my legs over the bannister and throw myself down to the floor below, landing on the daughter, laying, spent on the carpet like a drained whore, fondling herself gently, in some fucked up afterglow. I land feet first on the lower half of her torso, where she's more slug than person, and my feet disappear inside her. The burning is intense. Unbearable pain slides up my body. Hips on fire, as I roll to the side pulling myself from the thing, its guts over me. I can see my skin burning. Tendrils of smoke rising from me. I've fucked myself good and proper. Down to the carpet, blood slipping from my broken finger tips. My legs feeling like they're caught in a furnace, I drag myself through into the kitchen. The ones on the stairs turning. It seems the males are the only ones with the steam to move after the *fuckening*. Like they need to re-energise for another round, while the females just lay there, waiting. I kick at the door to shut it. Look around. I only have seconds.

If that.

I wasn't expecting to go out this way. I almost laugh at the thought. Christ. Whoever thought they'd go out this way? The window. It might be my only chance. I look at the wreck of my trousers. Burned through like I've had my legs dangling in a vat of acid. The skin showing below, raw and unflinchingly hot. I pull myself up the counter.

The door opens.

It's fucking Mr. T., looking for more action. I grab at the kitchen drawer and pull it open. Grab a knife from inside. It's a dinner knife, and absolutely no use whatsoever, but I'd rather have it, than not. I point it at T. I point it at the cock-thing looking at me. It's weird how even though it's a sausage with holes in it, I can still sense the desire to fuck me within it. "What the fuck do you want?" I look wildly around for something. Any-fucking-thing to get me a leg up on this bizarre and terrifying situation.

T. says, "Jeremy sends you all," in a dull hiss, something like a wheeze. "He always sends us gifts tonight."

I stare at the thing. No. Jerry couldn't have *known* this was going to happen. He couldn't have *known*. I shake my head, but the T. creature is nodding slowly, and I question why it would lie. Then that voice on my shoulder, you know, the one we all have says, *how does it know Jerry sent you?* We must have mentioned him, I answer it. Blinking. Frozen. The creatures behind T. now pulling at him, trying to get by him, to me.

But did we? Did we mention Jerry … like, at all? Fuck. I can't remember, but I stare T. in the face, and I don't know why, but I believe him. Shit. Jerry is back at the farm. With my wives. He could be doing anything.

Anything.

Fucker. I kick the door to the oven open. Pain thrashing at my legs. I only hope I can keep going. Lurching forward I turn the gas knobs. On the oven. On the hob. The hiss of the gas fills the room. And still they come. Like they can't smell it, or don't know. I don't know. I push myself up on the counter as the first of the males passes T., over him, into the room. Reaching for me, hands and proboscis. I reach back without looking and grab at the handle to the window. The stank of the gas filling my nose. The creatures coming. The smell of sex and rotting carcasses and shit filling the gaps in the room. The monsters unaware. I pull my lighter from my pocket and flick it open. The thing sparks as I roll back out the gap into the fresh air.

Whump.

The sound fills the air, as the gas and the oxygen from the window, the methane and God only knows what else in there fires. The following screams fill the silence of the night, as I lay there, tangled into a neatly trimmed rose bush.

Everything hurts. I pull myself out the Goddamned bush and crawl onto the lawn. The sound of the monsters in the burning house. The crackle of the house itself.

I'm out.

I made it. I glance back, but that's all I do. I'm not stopping. This suburban fucking neighbourhood is going to be alive with onlookers and coppers, the fire brigade. All in a matter of minutes. Half of them with their phones out filming this … *this*. The creature's howls fight for dominance over the roar of the fire. The smell of burning flesh … obvious.

I reach the side of the car, and lean against it for a second. Huffing air into my lungs. I can't believe fucking Jeremy had something to do with this. I feel like I've been run over. My legs are fucked, but I see lights in porches going on down the street. It's time I blew this joint.

I better head back to the farm. See *Jezza*. Find out what his deal was with these things. Fuck him up a bit.

No, scratch that.

Imma gonna head home, and get my wives to patch me up. Then I'm going to go to the workshop and find a chainsaw. *Then*, I'm going to go and see what he has to say for himself. Probably kill him. Cut him up into tiny pieces for cutting me and Johnny loose in a house of fucking monsters. That's fucking betrayal.

Betrayal, man.

Also, I checked. No. You can't buy bear traps on Amazon. But you can on Etsy, so maybe it was there?

NEXT LEFT

Even though the car was doing seventy, the burnt orange of the streetlights overhead moved slow across the bonnet, flashing through the car like strobes in a disco. Hayden looked at the radio, the time on it, nine-thirty. The song—he didn't know which one—stopped playing, down to an advert for the station. Didn't recognise it. It certainly wasn't a station from near home.

This is the news headlines, with Barbara Shannon.

The beat of the news program started. With each thump of the base vibrating through the car, Hayden's bladder hurt a little more. Shit. Well. Not shit … you know? He rested his elbow up on the edge of the window and pushed his hand into his forehead, taking the weight of his head. Sweat from his face, sticky on his fingers.

Evidence has emerged that the Roadside Killer has struck again. New Scotland Yard to comment.

He glanced to the briefcase on the passenger seat, swapping hands with the one on his head to the steering wheel and the one on the steering wheel to the case. Resting on it, like a child's blanket. Piss. It was morphing from a muscular pain to a burning pain. He was going to have to piss. Hayden looked down between his legs into the footwell of the Ford. There was the briefest of moments when he thought about just relaxing and letting the stuff dribble down his leg. But it wouldn't work like that, would it? It'd just soak in and he'd be sitting in pee for the next however long, and even after it dried out, he would still be able to smell it. He hadn't been looking after himself. He knew it. His wife knew. The GP. Everyone. He was dehydrated. He always was.

It would smell even worse.

London businessman Ewan Jafford's one-year-old son kidnapped, ransom demanded.

Both his hands now on the wheel, he looked out for some sort of signpost. Something to indicate there were a set of services coming. Damn it, he'd just been blindly following the GPS and he had no fucking idea where he was. He squinted at the orange hued world that surrounded the car. Pulled in to the left lane and under took one of those wankers that sat in the middle lane. Gave a quick glance as he passed the vehicle. Some geezer. Eyes fixed firmly on the road ahead. Looked about fifty. Probably thought he was a good driver. Pfft. Hayden leant over the car and popped the glove box open on the passenger side, pushing his hand in and smooshing it about, trying to find something to hold pee. Finding nothing, he sat back up. Came under the glowering rear lights of an eighteen-wheeler he'd nearly ridden up the arse of. He dropped his foot to the brake. Swung the car to the middle lane. Cleared his throat, pretending he hadn't nearly shit.

Prime Minister Jason Rogers to resign. Full stories on the hour.

Hayden took his eyes from the road again and scoured the floor of the car. There. In the passenger well. A water bottle. Rolling about over the empty McDonalds wrappers and chocolate bars.

The burning was unparalleled now. Maybe there was something really wrong with him? He peed not so long ago, right? Fuck. What was that thing you had that made you pee … prostitutes? No. Fucker. Don't be stupid. He ducked down. His hand barely on the wheel and grabbed the bottle. Sat back up, straightening the car before he veered off into the central reservation and rolled the thing, over and over. He looked at the bottle. Triumphant. Thumbed the lid off. He looked at the opening. About the size of a ten pence. There was no way he was fitting the end of his junk in there. He'd have to aim.

Hayden pushed himself down in his seat and clamped the steering wheel in between his knees. To keep the car straight. He was in the passenger seat once when a dude he was working with did it. Driving with his knees, that is, not peeing in a bottle. This dude had done it so his hands were free to roll a cigarette. It'd seemed stupid at the time. But now it was clear. It was genius. "Yes," he muttered to himself, as the song *Raining Men* started playing on the radio. He yanked down his fly and stuffed his hand in, wending it passed his girth, trying to find the end of it. Grabbed it. Pulled it out like a retractable dog lead. He pushed the end of his head up against the plastic of the bottle. It was surprisingly sharp. Then, he briefly wondered where the bottle had come from. He hoped it was his. Not some hitch hiker from down the road. Didn't want to catch something.

He looked out the window quickly, just to make sure this elaborate driving scheme he was running didn't have him drifting towards a bridge. Then back to the bottle. This was never going to work.

Yes. Yes it was, motherfucker.

He tried to relax. De-stiffen that muscle that was holding everything in. The one that didn't naturally want to relax. When sitting in the car. Driving. Peeing. Then it did a little. He felt the piss travel the length of his cock and then burst into the bottle.

Everything suddenly went horribly wrong. He had about as much control as a fireman with one hand on a fire hose. The head of his cock bulged, the bottle really wasn't big enough and the piss was firing back at him like a shaken champagne bottle. "Fuck," Hayden screamed, piss flying asunder. He squeezed his muscle back shut, cutting off the hose, and flailed in the seat. Realised he was no longer holding onto the steering wheel with any part of his body, dropped the bottle into the footwell, and pissily grabbed the steering wheel. Cock a-dangling. *Raining Men* stopped playing and some over hyped twat-waffle came on the air, talking about how the weather was going to change in the week ahead.

Hayden firmly kept one hand on the wheel, while the other wrestled himself back into his trousers. Left the zip down, though. Hard work zipping up when sitting.

Then he saw the sign.

Hot + Cold Food

1 Mile

It was a sudden relief. A weight lifted. Some sort of services. It wasn't one of those big brown signs, more of a half-arsed hand painted thing, but it was going to do. He dropped himself across the lanes to the left and sat there, rolling a clean seventy, and after less than a minute, another sign.

Hot + Cold Food
Next Left

Perfect. He said, "Wanker," and killed the radio. He glanced at the briefcase and used the sleeve of his suit jacket to mop pee from it. Then he pushed the button and brought the window down. The cold air of the night on the small gap. Sounded like a wind tunnel. The cool on his sweat-face. He saw the off, and indicated. The orange glow of the motorway lights not reaching from the central reservation to the ramp, disappearing. Suddenly the road only lit by the car headlights. Hayden flicked the switch on the stork and they went full beam.

The road was only one lane. He'd not seen anything other than the hand-painted signs, but he didn't care what was up there. So long as there was some sort of toilet.

He reached the top of the ramp and the space opened out before him. A small car park, and then the ramp going back down to the road. Shit. There wasn't a building. He pulled the car into one of the spaces. The car park lit by two or three small streetlights high above. The light from them barely reaching the tarmac. Hayden frowned around. A few cars dotted about. He squinted through the window into the car three spaces down. Empty. Opened the door and slipped his legs out. The numbness of the long drive, blood flowing hard back into them and he used one hand on the door to pull himself up to stand. He turned in a circle. Far side of the car park. There was a caravan set up. One of those burger van things. Side open like a food truck. Fine.

They must have a crapper there somewhere.

He reached into the car, leaning over the seat, and grabbed the briefcase. Pulled it out and slammed the door. Used the fob on the key to lock it. Jammed it into his trousers. He half-hurried across the car park. Doing a funny dance when his foot disappeared into an un-before-seen pothole. He looked into the car he was passing. Someone in there. Driver's seat. Head back. Sleeping. The windows of the car lightly fogged from the warmth inside.

Hot footing forward, he followed the lights to the … seating area? Hard to say. The caravan—and it was a caravan at one point—was obviously a permanent fixture. There were a selection—mish-mash—of garden furniture scattered around said seating area. Plastic chairs and tables, brought two at a time by the burger van owner, to create this Shangri-La in an unmarked off ramp on one of the busiest roads in the UK. Some geezer's own private Idaho. Kinda. He hurried from the car park to the seating area and weaved around the plastic chairs, the whole place looking like a ramshackle back garden barbeque.

The man, in the caravan. He was tall enough that you couldn't see the top of his head through the serving hatch cut in the side of the thing. It was sharp edged, and looked like someone had taken an angle grinder to the side of it, creating this Saw-like death trap that you had to reach through to get your …

Hayden looked quickly at the offerings.

… shit food. He reached the … opening. Ignoring the other patrons. Two at one table, and one at another. The one alone looked suspicious. Like they were trying to be as far away from other people as possible. "I need to pee," he said to the man.

The man looked at him like he was trying to process the statement. Like maybe he didn't speak English. Which wouldn't have surprised Hayden. Not really. He came from a small seaside town where half of the shops were run by migratory Eastern Europeans. Such nice people too. Hayden had stopped shopping in Tesco some time back, and only used smaller European supermarkets ... never mind. "I need to pee," he said, again. Fingers getting wet as the sweat rose on them, wrapped around the leather handle of the case. He glanced down at it. Then back up to the man. Frowning, still.

He was holding a spatula. Lifting it from the hot plate, he used it as a pointer, waving it in the direction of a path.

Hayden followed the point and then nodded a half-arsed thank you, before hurrying off in the direction of the path. As he got closer he could see. Not a path, but rather somewhere a number of people had trampled the foliage to nothing, a *desire path*. Not that he cared any longer. The burning in his gut was strong and he was going to piss. One way or the other, and he rather it not be inside his trousers. He already had pee stains on him from before. He glanced down at his shirt. Light stains there, *too*. He'd used a damp cloth but it hadn't all come out.

Hayden looked around. Realising he'd followed the path into almost complete blackness. He could still hear the sizzle of the hot plate, but he was now somewhere around the back of the caravan, hidden in the darkness. Seemed a bit ... seedy ... but fine. That was clearly where the chef (*chef, lol*) had indicated, and that was where he was going to pee. Hayden stood there for a moment, and stared into the black, waiting for his eyes to get used to the darkness. They didn't. He pulled his phone from his pocket. Eight missed calls. Great. He ignored them and flicked on the torch, illuminating the space he was in, so he knew where to aim.

The small circle of light bounced around as Hayden flashed it at the floor. The trampled pathway, giving to a small circle of dead ground. The toilet, apparently. Hayden looked at the shit on the floor. Various shades of brown through white. He looked to his feet. Trodden some of it in.

Burning though.

Didn't care. He looked to the side and put his case on a patch of dirt (mud, he hoped) and then pulled his fly. Unrolled his junk and waited. Wanted to pee so much, he had to wait for the muscles to relax. Still waiting. That fucking burning pain.

Then it came. A dribble at first. Heard it spatter to the mud in front of him. Then it came harder. The stream finally free of the muscle and he felt the urine as it passed below the surface of his skin, fingers wrapped around his cock. Movement of liquid. The sound of the spatter getting louder, he then flashed the torch in the direction he peed and saw the deep dark liquid in the blackness of the night rat-a-tat onto the edge of the *desire toilet*.

Waiting, he glanced around into the darkness. The sounds of the motorway were there on the edge of his hearing … barely audible over the nothing … the sizzle of the plate. He could smell his pee. But there was also the smell of cooking meat in the air, too. Made his stomach rumble. Shit.

The pee started to slow. He had a grip on his cock far enough down his shaft that he wasn't going to piss on his fingers, but he tried to aim away from his trousers. They'd already felt the wrath of far too much today. He flipped the light on the phone off and jammed it back in his pocket, then palmed his junk back in his trousers. The pain hadn't subsided none. Still burned.

It crossed his mind that it might not just be pee, and he might have *caught* something. He had fucked some girl last week, someone he picked up in the pub. Weird place to pick up a chick. He was in this old-timey fucking place, had a bed and breakfast attached to it— which was why he was there, and this young thing ... probably no more than seventeen ... she'd been in there pissed-up. She'd all but thrown herself at him. It wasn't like he had a choice.

Was it?

He shook his head, scooping up the case. Felt the weight of it, judging the contents, like it might have been tampered with while he was standing there next to it. No. He was sure that if he *had* caught something then he wouldn't be able to feel it yet. It'd be weeks before some STD became noticeable. Right? Christ. He shook his head. He had no idea.

Hopefully it was just the need to pee.

He started back along the desire path to the ... God. What do you even call this place? It was hardly a Comfort Inn, was it? Rounding the over growth, he could see the lights from the caravan. The smell, stronger.

He could hear the sizzle from the hot plate.

Hayden returned from the trampled path to the clearing, and looked quickly around the people at the table. Cautious, of them, and looking cautiously.

But the smell from the hot plate was strong, and his gut, free—well, freer—from the push of piss, grumbled. It wanted food. His eyes crawled over the couple. Then to the shadowed figure over the far side. He couldn't be sure if it was a man or a woman, but whoever … they hadn't moved while he'd been peeing. He tried to look casual while he went to the caravan. The man in there, flipped something, his eyes on Hayden though, not what he was doing.

When he was up close to the counter, the man pushed the spatula against the burger. It hissed like burning flesh does. The oil spat from it. The smell stronger. Then the spatula, underneath, a quick and graceful flip, and it was on the other side.

The man flipped it once more, and then scooped it up. From the heat. To a bun. Held it in a serviette like a taco shell, keeping his fingers from touching the bread. "Burger," he called.

Hayden looked at his fingers. Blackened by the heat. Sooty. They were leaving marks on the red serviette. The man was tall. Thin. He had no lips when he pursed his mouth hole together, and everything there at the edge of the caravan smelt like char. Burning. Heat. He took his eyes from the man and his fingers. The burger. He dropped them to the price list on the front of the caravan, below the opening. Took a step back to focus.

Not a price list.

Nothing had a price. Just the items. Like a menu in a fancy restaurant. If you have to ask how much it costs, you can't afford it. *That sort of place.*

Suddenly there was a woman standing there next to him. He glanced to her. She paid him no mind. Reached out and took the burger the man was holding. They met eyes briefly. She touched his fingers as she took it. Drew back, quickly. Burger in hand. Then she retreated. Hayden watching her go. She went back to the far corner. Into the shadows. She slunk. Slinked? Whatever. She was dressed provocatively. Unbefitting a motorway service burger van slab of grass, with included desire path pisser. Black dress. Looked *cocktaily*, for lack of a better word.

He wondered what sort of car she was driving, you know, to be able to slip in and out in a dress that didn't let her legs part properly. Also … how she went to the toilet …

The man cleared his throat. He looked at Hayden now. Standing there over the heat. His face was relaxed. He didn't look … anything. Expressionless, for the most part.

Hayden found it quite perturbing, drawing the case around in front of him. Holding it between his two hands, in front of his crotch. He stepped back up to the counter and the man spoke.

"What can I get for you?"

He had a soft voice. It surprised Hayden. He expected that standing over the heat like that wouldn't be good for the vocal chords. "What did she have?" he asked.

The man's eyebrow went up. "Doesn't matter," he said. "What do you want?"

Hayden frowned. He didn't like the man's tone. But his stomach growled again, and the burning pain in his bladder bloomed a little harder. Maybe eating something would help? Couldn't hurt. He glanced over the surfaces inside the caravan. Didn't look like Food Standards had checked the place out. He didn't really want to catch food poisoning from some fucking burger—

"What?" the man asked, cutting off his train of thought.

Hayden drew his eyes back to the man. He smiled. Didn't want to upset him. Not now. Not with … he let the case drop to the side, holding it in one hand again, properly, like a briefcase. A glance down to the menu he couldn't see at that angle. Then up. He was more than aware that he needed to make a decision. "Burger," he said. It was the only thing that came to mind.

The man nodded. He reached down, below the counter, then pulled out a slab of minced meat from down there, tossing it onto the hot plate. The meat thwapped down and let out this *chisssss*, before dying back quiet. "What else?" he asked.

Hayden shook his head. He still didn't know how much it was. As he was about to thrust his hand into his pocket and pull his wallet, the man said, "Go and take a seat. I'll call you when you can eat."

Hayden nodded again. Turned without word to the seating area. He glanced at the couple. There was a hotdog on the table in front of the man. Nothing in front of the woman. And they both stared at the dog. Weirdos. A glance back to the shadows to the woman with the burger. She was sitting again. He couldn't see what she was doing. Hidden in the shade. It was like she was holding the burger, without eating it.

What the fuck was wrong with the food in this place?

Hayden went and sat. A couple of tables across from the couple, the other side of the seating area from the woman, and facing the caravan. He rested the briefcase on the floor between his feet, and clamped them together to hold it there. Making sure he could feel it the whole time. The ground was dead. It looked like it used to be grass, maybe still there in some patches, but mostly it was dirt so dry it had cracked.

Surprising with the amount of rain they'd had recently.

Hayden looked to the sky. No stars or moon up there. Perhaps they hadn't had bad weather there. He was, after all, a long way from home. Easy done on the motorway. He stopped and listened. Between the pull off, and the walk to the seating area, he couldn't hear the road from there. The cars. It was peaceful.

Stomach growl. Christ. Where was his burger? He was starving. He stared, absently, at the man in the caravan. Not watching him cook the burger, just ... staring. He was flipping it back and forth like he'd done a million times before. Graceful in his movement. The *schlling* of the spatula scraping across the hot plate. Then the *chisssss* of the burger, launched for a split second to the air, then landing hard. Over and back. Over and back.

Bladder hurt.

Burger *chissss*ing.

He tapped his fingers on the plastic garden table. He looked at the desire path into the bathroom. Rested his hand down on his lower belly. Felt the muscle constrict slightly. Maybe a trip to the quack once this was all sorted out. Maybe he had a piss infection or something. Wanted to go again. Or perhaps that should be *still*. He could feel it there. You know. The muscles at the edge of the cock holding it there, instead of the one deep in the belly.

Oh God.

The words came from the woman in the darkness. Hayden turned in his seat. Feet off the case, but his hand down, instinctively to rest on it. And he looked, squinting into the dark. He could see her. She'd dropped the burger down onto the table. The top of it, the cap of the bun, it had fallen off, and it was rocking gently on the table. The other half, a chunk torn from it where she'd bitten it, resting half on the serviette and half off. Hayden watched. What was wrong with her? It? Was it the food? Was there something wrong with that?

"Burger," the man from the caravan called.

Hayden turned in his chair and looked at him. He was standing there. Fresh burger in his hand. Holding it. Blackened fingers on a red serviette. He looked back towards the woman. Then the couple. They had still to touch their hotdog. Sitting on the serviette. On the table. He glanced back towards the cars. They seemed so far away. The lights from the car park, dim in the distance.

"Burger," the man called again. This time he

sounded annoyed. Like he had something better to do.

It took Hayden's attention and he pushed himself to stand. Took the case. Went to the caravan. He still didn't know how much the thing was, not that he had any particular want to find out now. As he walked he glanced down at the hotdog on the table. It looked like any other hotdog. But the woman's face was all screwed up like it was shit in a bun. The man with her, his arm around her, comforting her. Hayden looked back, the way his feet were carrying him. Hand going into his jacket, he took the wallet from inside and pulled it. "How much?" he asked.

The man in the caravan looked vague. "Your money's no good here, son," he said.

Hayden snorted. "Son, right. How much?"

The man thrust the burger forward. "Take it," he said.

Hayden stood, listless for a moment. Then he pushed his wallet back in his jacket. Reached out and took the burger, fingers on the red serviette. He brushed the blackened skin of *his* fingers. They were hot. From the fire, presumably. But sticky, hot. Hayden took the burger. Fingers pushing into the bun, soft, the other side of the tissue of the serviette. He nodded his thanks to the man.

Went to turn, when the man stopped him.

"What's in that case of yours?"

Hayden stopped. He didn't turn back. Just turned his head. Looked at the man. Then dropped his eyes to the case in his hand.

"You just seem awfully attached. Ain't no one

gonna take it from you here," he said. "You're with friends."

Hayden eyed him suspiciously, but quickly. The idea in his mind that he might know what was in the case suddenly at the forefront of his head. He frowned, and then shook his head at him. He tried to convey that the contents of the case was unimportant, and that he shouldn't worry about things that were not of his concern, but all it seemed to do is raise a smile on the man's face. Hayden turned away, clinging onto the burger and returned to his seat. The woman at the table being held by her partner, was crying now.

Hayden stopped and looked. The hotdog didn't look great, but it certainly didn't look that bad. Not crying about it bad. Then he felt a pang of pity for the poor man that had cooked it, watching this woman, who not only refused to eat it, but also cried over it, like it was spilled milk.

He took a glanced to his own hot food. The serviette was dampening with the grease that ran from it. Slippery on his fingers. Then he sat. Looked at the man in the caravan, watching. Movement in the corner of his eye, Hayden turned his head. He looked. Saw the woman from the other table in the far corner get up and stride towards the rest of them.

She seemed to suddenly have purpose.

Hayden absently bit into his burger, without thinking. Like popcorn on social media. About to kick off. *Something* was about to happen.

The flavour of the burger melted into his mouth. It was a strange consistency, but in that split second he wondered how cheap the meat had to be to be sold at that price.

Free.

But it tasted wonderful.

The woman from the far table reached the couple at the table in the middle and swung her arm back.

This was it. The *something* that was about to happen was happening. Hayden couldn't take his eyes from it. It was *enthralling*.

Her arm swiped back, all a blur, and it looked for all Hayden was worth that she was punching the other woman in the back of the head. But she didn't. Her hand came to a stop at the back of the woman's neck. The front of her neck spiked out, and was pierced. Hayden's eyes widened as a small drool of blood came from the woman's neck.

The other woman—slinky—she pulled the thing out.

Hayden saw. It was a pen. A fucking biro. His eyes went to the woman again. With the pen withdrawn blood spooted out of the wound in her neck, like some sort of reverse tracheostomy. A small chew on the meat in his mouth and Hayden discarded the burger in his hand. Went to stand.

There were two hands, firmly placed down on his shoulders, specifically to stop him.

"Isn't she *wonderful?*"

The voice, coming from behind him was that of the man in the caravan. Hayden stopped, and swallowed his meat. Almost getting it stuck in the surprise, the shock. Choking. Swallowed, though. And fine. He looked up, over the back of his head. Saw the man there. He could see his chin. Up his nose.

He looked back to the caravan, wondering how he'd managed to get there that fast, and perhaps, that silently. The caravan, gone.

Hayden frowned.

Looked back at the woman holding the biro. Then the other one. The one that was bleeding. Gushing, she was now. The blood firing from her with a force that even Hayden hadn't seen before. The blood coming forth like a geyser on the flats of some hitherto never before visited plain somewhere. The white garden furniture splattering deep red.

The woman looked pretty surprised, to be honest.

The colour draining from her face.

Also, the man with her looked a little bewildered, too.

She spluttered, airways blocked, and blood spat from her mouth. Drooling down her chin like vomit from a pisshead.

Hayden frowned. He clamped his fingers a little tighter around the handle of the briefcase. Looked at the woman's face for the first time. The one standing. The one ... not bleeding to death. She was stunning, in that old fashioned porcelain doll sort of way. Skin that looked like it was stretched over a mannequin. Her eyes, though, they were deep. Startling. Dark. Black. Something you could fall into. An abyss. Hayden realised the abyss was looking back. He smiled, the hands of the man behind him still on his shoulders. He felt like he could have tried to move. Maybe push himself from the man's grip and get to stand, but he was in the middle of a game of chess it appeared.

One he was an unwilling participant in.

He looked back to the missing caravan. Rather, he looked back to the where the caravan should have been. His frown deepened. He wasn't into magic tricks. Never had been. This Magic Mike ... no wait, that wasn't right ... Paul Daniels shit didn't impress him. He could still hear the sizzle of flesh. The smell of cooking meat. It was all smoke and mirrors. He looked to the woman whose gushing had eased now, as she did a quick shudder and flopped forward, her head bonking on the plastic table. The hotdog bouncing slightly like it was on the other end of a see-saw. Bonk. Jump. Hayden looked at the theatrics occurring around him. He'd walked into the middle of some travelling magic show. Like that Richard Layman book. Except they were vampires weren't they?

That was it.

"Very good," he said. He tried to move. Just gently. Wasn't trying to force the hands from him. Just wanted to get up and thank them for the show and leave.

Quickly.

But the grip of the man behind him was strong. Stone-like. He pushed Hayden back into his seat. His blackened fingers massaging the muscles, taut around his clavicle. The man leant closer.

"What's in the briefcase, Hayden?" the man whispered. His mouth down, close to his ears.

The woman. Holding the biro. "Yes. What's in the case?"

There was a sudden and harsh stabbing in Hayden's bladder. He let his free hand move to it. Cup it. Caress the pain away.

"It won't be long now," said the man behind him.

"What?" Hayden said the word so quietly it did nothing more than come from his mouth as a breath. Without waiting for an answer though, Hayden continued. "I need to pee again."

The man's fingers seemed to ponder on his shoulder for a moment. Then he released him. "The desire path," he said.

Hayden listened to him step back, away from him, and released, he stood. He glanced back to the car park. So far away. He felt like he could run for it. But that woman. She was slender and lithe. Surely fitter than he. He was a gelatinous blob that wanted nothing more than to be loved. But no one ever wanted him because … Hayden stopped himself. *Enough of that*, he thought. Time for self-hate later. He took the briefcase, and decided the best thing to do was to go to the piss hole. He looked at the man behind him as he circled. Had an apron on. *Stan's*. The name of the burger van. He hurried towards the desire path and in. Into the darkness. He stumbled back, around, and to where he was before. In the darkness. Unlit. He felt the damp of the ground squidging around his shoes, his feet. "Damn," Hayden muttered. He hoped in his haste he hadn't stumbled too far and was now ankle deep in piss and … whatever else people had been doing around there. "Fucking desire path," he said to himself. He stopped moving and took in a breath. The stench of piss, mixed with the smell of cooking. He pulled his phone and thumbed the torch on. This time paying more attention to the ground. The trodden down grass and undergrowth, dark and sticky. "Shit." He snorted to himself. Flashed the light around his feet. The ground black. He looked closer. Crouched. The pain inflaming in his gut as he bent. He looked down into the mire of piss. Shit. And something else. His natural reaction to reach forward and stick his fingers in the unknown substance and *test it*, but he stopped himself. Stupid. Sticking fingers in shit. Closer, though, the smell changed, and the pee wasn't the strongest thing. It was something else. He looked at the briefcase. His hand still wrapped around the handle, it was resting next to him. Perhaps it was that, he could smell?

The piss stab hit him again and he stood. Phone back in his pocket. He held the case in one hand this time and got his cock out with the other. Stood there for a moment. Nothing forthcoming. Shit. If he'd picked something up …

He pushed his cock back in his trousers. All he had to do now was circle the edge of the seating area and head back to the car. Forget about the travelling circus out there. Get back in the car and leave. Pee over himself if he had to. Had to be better than this. He stumbled back along the path and to the edge of the opening. Stopping while he was still in the shadows. Things had changed. The man, Stan. He was standing, watching. The woman with the biro. She was standing behind the man who was with the woman. The one with the new neck vent.

And he was standing over *vent-neck*.

While Hayden was in the pisser, for lack of a better term, they'd moved the 'dead' woman. Slumped her over the table. Now, the man she was with was fucking her from behind. The woman with the biro, behind him, biro to the side of his neck. All the while Stan was watching.

It was obviously part of the act. All for Hayden's own benefit, of course. Although the guy fucking the 'dead' woman was putting his heart and soul into the act. His tears glistened in the moonlight, Hayden could see them from where he observed. He was crying out, between thrusts. The dead woman had her skirt up, over her torso. Panties down to her knees. Her body rocked without musculature integrity as he stuck her like she was a fruit pie. The table rocked with each of his thrusts. "Please," he cried. "Don't. I can't."

"Oh, but you can," said Stan. He leant forward. Hands went down to rest on the table, in fists. One each side of the dead woman's head, as it rocked back and forth. His voice was deeper than before. "Do it," he whispered. "Do it now."

The man was grunting. Harder. He was fucking her harder. Pushing. Desperately trying to finish.

Hayden squinted. He looked by them to the car park. There was no way in Hell he was going to get from where he stood to the car without at least one of these freaks seeing him. He returned his look to the ... *circus*.

"Come on then," barked Stan.

Hayden nearly laughed out loud.

"Now."

Then the man started to grunt properly. Hard. Like he was about to ... you know. *Come on then*. The man started to judder. The process of the orgasm gripping him while he was still inside the corpse. Pretend corpse. Obviously.

Then he pulled out. Jizz firing uncontrollably up the back of the woman. Coming out the guy like he was on little blue pills. Stan stepped back. Away from the hose fire. The man wailed out in what sounded far more like pain than pleasure, as he stumbled back, into the body of the waiting woman. The biro held to his neck.

Cock pointing to God. White, sticky juices still flowing from the end.

Stan was laughing at the man's disgust. His face contorted to horror. Cheeks wet with tears.

"It's time to move on …" Stan waved his hand dismissively. The woman with the biro, releasing the man and backing away. And he was left standing there, over the woman.

Hayden caressed his gut. Pretty sure that it was getting worse.

The man held his hand out towards Stan. Like he was waiting for him to give him something, then he cried out in pain. A loud crack cut across the seating area. And his scream rose an octave.

The man's leg snapped backwards at the knee like an animals. His yell filling every inch of the space. Like a void in space filled suddenly with the screams of the damned. His legs out from under him, he fell to the compressed dirt below, dry and cracked.

Hayden could barely make out the words hugged within the screams … something about *no*, and *please*. The man reached forward for the ground. His leg splitting open as the broken bones tore the flesh asunder. Blood spilling forth, thick and wet. Glistening. The man looked at his leg, his hands tenderly coming to aid the destroyed limb, but then stopping as he realised sticking his fingers into the mush of flesh was pointless. Stupid, even. He looked up to Stan, then back to the woman. The screams gone, momentarily, like he forgot the pain existed. His hand snapping back on itself. The bones underneath the skin snapping, as that contorted. Fingers splayed and useless as the muscles tore. Bone shards sticking from the flesh. The screaming began again. The man screamed, "I don't deserve this."

Stan smiled. "Of course you do," his reply.

Hayden's face curled into a gurn as he watched the man, writhing at first, then as his other leg was shattered by some force he couldn't see, he buckled into a traction position, back curled. Afraid to move for the pain it would bring.

Stan looked from the man, to Hayden, apparently not as hidden in the darkness as he thought. "Time is catching up," he said.

Hayden stepped out. A quick look to the car park. It seemed so very far away. As he approached the carnage on the floor. The corpse of the woman, slumped over the table. The man's liquid life spitting from his body as it continued to tear, gushing out from some places, firing out like a squirt gun from others. He twisted and turned, the screams gone, the pain his everything now. Hayden stopped, long before he was close enough to get the man's blood on him. He could smell the rotten stank of the metals in the blood.

Sure, now, this was no circus.

"Who are you?" Hayden asked.

"What's in the case?" Stan said.

Hayden gripped the case harder. The pain shooting across his gut making him caress it again. There was a new smell in the air. Amid the stink of the man's flesh and cum … the smell of the cooking meat, from the burger van that no longer existed. There was a smell he couldn't quite place. Cigarettes, perhaps. He used to smoke. That smell was quite the delight to him. But it was acrid. Like an ashtray, sat in a whore's bedroom for too long. He glanced towards the man, still breathing, bleeding. Bits of him removed from the whole now. An unseen force tearing chunks off him. Pulling the flesh from the bones, but leaving just enough to let him stay, alive, conscious, to witness the pain. Blood drooling from his mouth, choking. Spluttering.

Hayden shook his head. He walked to the table where the woman lay. Lifted the case to the flat surface next to her and put it down with some reverence. He eyed Stan. Then his look to the woman. "I … think I see where this is going," he said.

Stan smiled. "Sharp," he said.

"But I don't understand her." He looked back to Stan. Eyes in his. Making sure that Stan knew he meant it.

"She's a serial killer. What do you expect?"

Hayden shrugged. He popped open the briefcase and looked at the contents. Each hand on the corner of the open case. A small smile. Admiring his previous handiwork.

"Can I see?" Stan asked.

Hayden looked up to him. Down to the case. He

didn't really want to share. At least, part of him didn't. There was a part that wanted everyone to see the contents of the case. But he knew it must be kept a secret. It had to be.

"It doesn't matter now," Stan said.

Hayden's eyes fell to the case. He was right, clearly. He turned the case on the table like he was some big shot in the movies, showing the drug dealer the case of money, except it wasn't a drug dealer and the case had a cut up baby in it. The child's skin white. The blood sloshing in the bottom of the case. Thickening. Clotting.

Stan raised an eyebrow. "And so you know why you're here."

Hayden nodded. "Yeah," he said, slowly. "I don't know how though." He looked down at the body of the man. Still alive. Just twitching now. His eyes wide open. Mouth moving, but nothing coming out. His skin burned from his body, bones broken. But he wasn't dead.

Well ... technically, he was.

But here, in this rest stop, conscious and well enough to feel everything that Stan smited on him.

Stan gestured to the man on the ground. "It was their Silver wedding anniversary. She was giving him head in the car. Caused the whole thing. Part of the steering column impaled her while she was still gobblin' him up. He was broken up in the car, when they hit the central reservation." Stan sighed. "Lost control when he nutted."

Hayden nodded. "Got both of us in the cross fire?"

he asked.

"Yep. You went straight up their rear. Pushed the front end of the car up, the block pushing the steering wheel straight into your torso."

Hayden looked at the woman. Didn't have a scratch on her. "And her?"

"She's still in limbo. The car is upside down. Petrol leaking from the tank. She's unconscious. The petrol will drown her. But I like her without the scars. Might throw her a bone later," he said, winking at Hayden.

The pain in his stomach pushed again. He let his hand drop from the case to his gut. Felt the sticky warm of blood there. "It's time," he said.

"It is."

"It's going to hurt?"

"Very much."

Hayden took one last look at the banker's baby. Knew he should have just taken the ransom instead of letting his more ... base ... instincts take over. Should have just left the hatchet-jobs for the whores. He shook the thought away. Too late now. He looked back to the car park. It was gone. They now stood on an island of ground in the midst of a blackness of nothing surrounding them.

The woman started to cough.

The smell of cigarettes was stronger. It overtook most of the other smells now. Sulphur. Hayden watched the woman. She spewed out, petrol coming from her maw like puke. Like she'd been pulled from the sea, and some life guard had thumped her chest, water ejecting. She clawed at her throat, unable to breathe. Her lungs burning. The petrol spilling down her as she vomited it out. But she couldn't expel enough of it to clear her lungs, no matter how many times it came from her.

She dropped to her knees. The look in her eyes. Hayden took a step closer. His one hand on the wound in his gut. The gash, he could feel it there now. He watched her eyes plead for forgiveness … perhaps … no …

… mercy.

As she drowned in petrol. Kneeling in a man's insides. Torn from his charred body.

Hayden looked at Stan. "Stan," he said. "Very droll."

Stan smiled. "I try. You'll get used to my sense of humour."

The darkness closed further around them as the woman stopped moving. The Roadside Killer, Hayden recalled. The hot liquid that surrounded his bladder slipped over his fingers, as his bladder dropped from inside his body to inside the palm of his hand. The pain, unbearable. "You've got to be shitting me," he whispered. "So why this?" He waved around to the seating area, now, nothing more than a patch of light in a black darkness of nothing.

Eternity of night.

Stan shrugged. "I mean, what's more appropriate? Do you know how many people get food poisoning from badly cooked burgers at these things?" He started to laugh.

The darkness was all encompassing Hayden now.

He was passing out. Passing over. He had no doubt he'd see Stan again.

Shortly.

THIS ONE DOOR

Dance picked up the torch from the concrete step, the beam cutting the darkness as he tested it, up, over the front door, and then down, to the lock. Malik was staring at him.

"Do you mind?" Malik asked.

Dance shrugged. "What?" he whispered.

Malik held the lock-picks in his hand, inches from the lock itself. He looked back to the street, over the tops of the grown out grass, to the wrought iron work of the fence. The street was still. It always was down there. There was little for anyone in the cul-de-sac. A couple of houses owned by the rich. Well, *richer*, at least. The whole town was broken down, little more than a drug haven. Unemployment rampant. Scum sitting on the pavement in every street. Urchins and beggars in the doorways before they were moved on. Totalitarian policing … when they could be bothered. He realised that Dance was staring at him. Eyebrows up. Waiting for him to pick at the lock. "Sorry," he muttered, sliding the two pieces of metal into the old Yale lock.

He wasn't exactly good at it, but the lock would come for him in a couple of minutes.

Malik twisted and turned the spikes of metal, feeling for the touch point. He was surprised when they had checked the place out earlier in the day that it had locks like this. The whole house was a surprise. From the road it looked like the house was abandoned, what with the front garden untended. A large detached property, so you could see down the sides of it. Over grown, pathways disappearing under grass that yawned out from the lawn. Coming to the front door and knocking was a no brainer. The same old scam. Find a house that looked good enough to turn over. Knock on the door in the middle of the day. If no one answered, quickly check out the windows and see if there was something worth stealing. If someone did answer, then they were from the council. *There had been reports of a smell of gas in the road, and was it okay to look around the outside of the property?* Never ask to go in. That was when anyone that was half-savvy would ask for some proof of I.D., which granted, wasn't often. Anyway. If you didn't ask to go in, half the time they didn't care if you looked around outside. It meant you could go around the windows and see what the house was like anyway.

Sometimes they would invite you in, regardless. Bored, and wanted company. Maybe interested in the report. If they invited you in then they *never* asked for I.D., so win-win.

No one had answered the door when they'd knocked that afternoon, and after a quick check in the windows, Malik had seen that it wasn't as dilapidated on the inside as the outside might have suggested, in fact quite the opposite. It looked almost hedonistic. Quite inappropriate living for a town like this. And there was a pile of post inside the front door. You could see it from the side window. The owners, clearly away.

There was no sign of alarm boxes on the outside of the building. No dog doors or shit in the garden. No visitors to the street while they were there.

It was a gimme.

So they'd come back.

The house lay in darkness and they were free to

work.

The lock clicked as it opened, and Dance turned the handle, waiting for Malik to carefully pull the picks from the lock and push them back into his breast pocket. Malik glanced once more to the deserted street, then nodded his head, still crouching. Dance pushed the door open, gently. He wanted to move the post without making noise. He was listening for movement.

They both listened for an alarm. Just because there were no boxes on the outside, didn't mean the street wasn't about to light up with flood lamps, sirens … you never knew what was going to happen when you actually found somewhere rich to break into.

But there was nothing.

Malik smiled and pulled his own torch as Dance pushed the door open. Malik almost squatting as he crab walked in. Low. Silent. Dance followed, stepping over the post and pushing the door closed. The two of them in the house. Darkness. There was a smell. Smelled like death. Rotting. Something dead. Dance joined Malik, near to the ground. "What do you think?"

"That smell," Malik said. "Stinks. Reckon there's a dead body in here?"

Dance glanced down to the post. "Maybe a week? Could be. You'd think someone would have found him by now."

Now it was Malik's turn to shrug. "Yeah." He flashed his torch around the hallway. It was one of those rich people hallways. Open. Table in the middle. Vase on it. Dead flowers. The hardwood floor had been polished to within an inch of its life. The wallpaper was old fashioned. Nothing looked … modern. "Old people," he muttered.

It bode well for them. It was only eleven at night. If the owner was lying in bed having died in their sleep, they had all night. Which was pretty much perfect. A Wednesday night. There wasn't likely to be any traffic in the closed off road, the neighbours long in bed for work the next day. They could probably turn the lights on.

"Find the smell, first," he said, continuing his thoughts out loud like Dance could hear them.

"Gotcha." Dance flashed his light to the stairs. "I'm going up," he whispered, moving silently in the darkness. He went to the stairs, and gently started up. Walking to one side, pigeon walking as close to the bannister as he could so there was less likelihood of chance floorboard noise. Not that a house like this probably had creaky stairs. Probably.

Malik waited for Dance to reach the first landing—yes, it was that sort of stairwell—and when he turned to the left to continue up, Malik took stock of the hallway. The house was double fronted, so he expected a living room on one side, and a dining room on the other, however they'd organised those, kitchen at the back, and a wash room. Something like that. He was still crouching. Knees aching slightly. He pushed himself up, hand on knee to stand. He'd been suffering with his knees for some time. Getting old.

Over to the room on the right. From the window outside it looked like the living room, although it was little more than quick glances earlier. The smell dissipated as he went through the open arch doorway. No dead body in there, that was for sure. Straightening a little, he felt safer. Went to the armchair that faced away from the window and flashed the torch light into it. Just to be sure. He didn't know why he almost felt a pang of relief when there wasn't a dead body there. Calming, he checked around the room. The chair looked old, like an antique, and not even particularly comfortable. Just expensive. Which was a good sign, all things considered. He even let himself smile. The chair faced the TV. Didn't recognise the brand, but it was huge. Curved slightly. Malik didn't know shit about TV's but it looked expensive. No fucking way they were shifting it though. Fine. Everything seemed to be oozing money, so he just needed something manageable in size. Jewellery was his first thought. He heard a creak above his head. Dance landing a floorboard. If he'd told him once about being careful. Malik shook his head, torch flashing quickly around the room.

As he expected them to have all night, he wanted to check the house for living people first, so he left that room. Back to the hallway and straight across. Into the one opposite. Again the smell dispersing as he entered.

They hadn't been able to see into there from outside, so he was more careful. Glancing in around the frame of the archway first, just to be sure there wasn't some ancient old man standing there with a farmer's shotgun pointing him right in the chest. Which there wasn't. This wasn't their first rodeo after all. Malik let the torch light slip over the contents of the room. It was a sitting room at one end, diner at the other. So the kitchen *was* at the back. Behind the stairwell, he thought, and there was a doorway back there. It checked. The sitting room had bookshelves. Looked like the old man was a reader. Books had value. You didn't do this for years without learning that, but Malik also had no idea the difference between a valuable book and a charity shop book, so he barely let the light touch them. Rows of them, tidy, in shelves, a single chair in the middle of it all. Wingbacked. Looked in place. Expensive. One chair again, he thought. Good. So far, everything suggested that there was a single person living in this vast abode, and the smell suggested the old fart had dropped dead.

Heading towards the back of the room, he left the sitting area, an old-fashioned writing bureau under the window. He made a mental note to check through it once the house was clear. There was a photo on top of it. A man and a woman. Both grey haired and smiling. Looked like a photoshoot grandparents would have been gifted by their grandkids who never came visiting, one for their *whatever* wedding anniversary. He stroked the light across the picture frame and to the dining table. There was a plate on it. A single setting, although two chairs had been drawn out. The plate was mostly clean. It had been there for some time. No smell, but there was mould on the remnants of the last supper. Malik flashed the light between the four chairs, two in, two out. Then the single setting. A wine glass. Empty. Malik frowned. Who comes to someone's house and watches them eat? *Fucking rich people*. He turned the light to the door at the back of the room, closed. There was a farm-like sideboard next to it. Decorative plates. That sort of thing. Drawers. Cupboards below. Mentally noted. Going to the door, he put his gloved hand against the wood of it, pushing lightly. A smell coming from within. It wasn't good. Definitely not good. But it also wasn't dead person bad. In, he let the door swing closed behind him. Sure now, that the house had to be empty. High-end kitchen equipment littered almost every surface. Not what he had expected at all. He thought it would be a farm kitchen. Expected fancy wooden chopping boards and a deep inset sink, but instead finding the profusely lavish kitchen of a money rich young person. His torch settled on the sous vide machine. A money rich young person that had watched too many episodes of Masterchef. He slid the torch quickly around the room again, then went to the opposite door to the one he'd come into. He frowned. So, the living room must have been smaller than the sitting room. He tried to map the house in his head, but it didn't quite make sense to him. Tricks of the darkness, as he moved half blind without doubt.

The door opened to a bathroom, not the utility room he was expecting. Gold taps, and luxurious bathing equipment. Looked like something from the Titanic. Old. But rich. Didn't suit the outside of the property at all.

Fucking rich people, he thought, again.

He heard movement upstairs. Dance must have found something. He wasn't being quiet anymore. Malik went from the door of the bathroom back through to the dining room, to the hallway, his torch bouncing off anything that caught his eye. Dance was on the stairs. "You should probably come and have a look," he said. He motioned with this torch, the beam lighting the way up the stairs, to a single door. Above the kitchen.

He wasn't whispering.

As Malik climbed the stairs the stank of the dead got stronger. He joined Dance on the first landing as he waited, reluctant to move on alone. Then as Malik climbed, Dance walked behind him. "First door," he said. "That one." Malik headed towards the door that Dance had the beam of his torch on. Illuminating the white gloss painted wood.

Malik tread carefully still, although he could hear Dance behind him almost stomping. He reached the door and touched the handle. "What is it?" he asked, his eyes meeting Dance's own. Dance shrugged.

Malik pushed the door open, his shoulder against it. He led into the room with his torch light.

The bedroom.

An ornate four-poster bed sat against one wall, light curtains surrounding it. There was an oil painting on the wall opposite. The painting was of a port, a huge picture, within a gilded frame. Enormous wardrobes lined the other wall, dark oaks and walnuts. Eclectic and beautiful, the room was a mausoleum of fine furniture from the past. Although, the room neither seemed right, somehow, nor smelled particularly fine. It smelled of old meat. A butchers shop on a hot weekend, the last of the flesh hanging in the window, browning from the air touching it, the kiss of the sun.

Malik looked to Dance. He raised his eyebrows in question. A slight shake of the head, what? Dance flashed his torch to the four-poster. "There," he whispered.

Malik shook his head. He was whispering again. *Jesus*. He went to the bed and pulled the curtain to the side. Beneath was a woman. She lay on the bed, the sheet covering nothing of her naked flesh above the waist. Unmoving. Dead to the eye. He glanced back to Dance who just stood there. Still near the door, staring. Malik flashed his torch over the woman.

He was expecting someone of age, from the décor and look of the house ... the feel. But the body was that of a young woman. The torch on her face, Malik guessed her to be little more than twenty. His torch light tracing a silhouette of her naked body. She was stunning, at least in life, and Malik wasn't one for sentiment, but he felt his heart drop a little knowing that the world had lost this beauty.

She still looked good, although, now with the curtain pulled back, he could tell that the smell was definitely coming from her. "She's not been dead long," he said, judgment made by how little she had rotted. He waited, Dance not replying.

Then she moved. She juddered. Shuddered. Her lips opened a little, air escaping from them carrying a whine. Almost unperceivably quiet. Malik stepped back, almost falling.

He shot a look to Dance. What was he thinking? There was a fucking person, there, in front of them. If she was to awaken, then they'd have to kill. Or run. Both.

"It's okay," Dance said. "That's all she does."

Malik looked from Dance to the woman again. He held the light on her face. She was dreaming, perhaps, her eyes moving under the thin flesh of her lids. Another twitch. A tongue flick from beneath her lips, full, over them. Moistening them. Before she rested once again. It was like she was dreaming the most perfect dream. But couldn't wake up. "What the fuck is it?"

"I don't know." Dance reluctantly came to his side. "But she sure smells dead."

She did.

Malik reached forward and took the sheet in his hand, pulling it back, revealing the rest of the woman. She lay in stained sheets. It looked like the sheets had been pissed on, shit. Other fluids, too. The woman was wet, her mound slicked with her own juices.

Dance gagged. He backed away. "What the living fuck, man?"

Malik dropped the sheet back over her. He pulled the curtain back, so he couldn't see her. Smell her, quite so much. "We should call an ambulance."

Dance just stared at him blankly for a moment. "A-what now?" He took a fistful of Malik's jacket, taking him quite by surprise. "And tell them what? You know, me and my pal happened to be passing … the bedroom … and noticed this sickly individual. Who, by the way, looks in perfect health, although, may or may not have been in a coma for several weeks?"

Malik stared at him. "I see what you're saying." He brushed Dance's hand from him. "But we can't just leave her there, like that. Can we?"

"I can."

Malik dropped his head to the side. "Prick," he whispered. Loud enough that Dance would have heard, of that much he was sure. "All right," Malik continued. "We find what we can, take what we can. Call an ambulance after."

"You do what you want."

Malik watched as Dance walked away, across the bedroom to the wardrobes giving the bed a very wide berth. He pulled the doors open, dropping the backpack from his shoulder and started to rummage. Malik then pulled the curtain back and looked at the woman again. She was stunning. Closer, he could see a light film of sweat sheening her whole body. She wasn't atrophied. Wasted. She didn't even *look* hungry. She just wasn't moving. And smelled like she had been that way for some time. But Dance was right. He let the curtain go again, and turned back. Out the room.

Onto the landing. They used to have all night. He didn't feel like they did anymore. Get this done, and get out. If it was up to him, he'd already be on the phone, hot footing it down the street towards the main road.

He hurried down the stairs, torch light bouncing as he moved. Turned into the dining room come sitting room. Went to the drawers on one of the cabinets. Photo on top. He looked at the picture again as he pulled the top drawer. The man and woman. Something about them. Her. He squinted, arching in a little closer, but snapping out of it, as a noise upstairs brought him back to where he was. He focussed on the drawer. Full of jewellery. Pearls and diamonds. Necklaces. Earrings. They'd hit the jackpot, for sure. Malik dropped his pack to his feet, and started to feed the valuable trinkets in, slipping them away. It was all his now. His and Dance. A glance to the photo, then back to the job in hand. He emptied the drawer quickly, taking fist full after fist full of jewels, packing the bounty away. Opened the next drawer down, it was same. Again, overflowing with cubic zirconia, gold, silver.

He stopped. A handful of riches. Looked at the picture. Then his hand. He dropped them back. Into the drawer. Something wasn't natural. No one had this. Not here. Not like this. A young woman in a house, every orifice crammed with valuables. It wasn't ... right. It didn't look, or *feel* right. His stomach felt hollow. A sickness down in there somewhere. Even his body telling him that something was wrong.

The only thing he could think was to get Dance, and get out.

He picked his pack up and went to the stairs. He could hear Dance on the other side of the house now. A light on in the room opposite the one with the woman in, stealth discarded. He was being loud. Reckless. Careless. Malik went upstairs, two steps at a time. To the first landing, then up to the first floor. He opened the door with the light on.

Dance was hunched over a chest of drawers, using two hands to ladle gold chains into his backpack.

"Dance," Malik hissed.

He didn't stop. Didn't even look up. "What?" he snapped. "Have you seen this lot? The fucking motherlode."

"It's not right," Malik said. He flashed his torch over the landings and onto the stairs, standing in the doorway, half watching Dance. His greed pushing him forward.

"We've been doing this shit for years, and now ... now ... you get a conscience."

"No, listen." Malik watched Dance pushing this stuff into his pack. A bottomless pile of metal. It was going to be too heavy to lift, surely. "Don't you see? Everything is wrong here."

"Look," Dance stopped for the first time and glanced over to him, breathless. "You do you, okay? You got a boner for the girl ..." he shrugged. "Go fuck the girl—"

"It's not that," Malik snapped, cutting him off. "Don't you get it? The drawers full of money. The woman? Everything in here is ... perfect."

Dance stopped again and looked at him. He shook his head. "So you've lost it. Fine." He stood, picking up the bag and swung it back over his shoulder. "So let's go." It took him a minute to walk across the room to Malik. He stopped. Patted him on the chest. "Did you get much?"

"Too much," Malik whispered.

Dance snorted. "Okay. Let's shoot." He passed, went to the stairs and started down.

Malik watched him, tracing his steps with the torch. "Are you okay?" He didn't seem okay. He seemed like he was a man possessed a moment ago, one who had just been given a personality transplant.

"Cool," Dance replied, heading down towards the front door. He started whistling a tune. Something almost mournful.

"Stop," said Malik.

"What?" Dance replied. "I thought you wanted to leave?" He slowed, but didn't stop. Malik turned, flashing his torch into the room behind him, a sudden itchy feeling of someone there watching him. Something. His breathing became harder, his heart beating a half-step quicker, he turned back.

Dance was gone.

"Damn it," he mumbled, following the bannister along to the stairs and going down, to the front door. If Dance was being belligerent, then he could go fuck himself. He grabbed the handle and twisted. The door didn't move. Locked. "Damn it, Dance," he shouted, far too loudly, being as most of the house was still neck deep in darkness. Why had Dance locked the front ... his thoughts swayed. How had he? He patted his pocket, the picks still there. He was the only one with them. He shone the torch to the side rooms. Maybe he hadn't left. "This isn't a fucking joke," he hissed out in the darkness.

"No," came the voice from behind him. Back, and up. On the stairs.

Malik turned. It certainly wasn't Dance on the stairs behind him judging by the voice. Shadowed in the half-light of the room on the first floor, Malik pointed his torch at him. It sounded like a him anyway, as he stumbled back seeing the visage before him. A tall figure, probably a man, bereft of skin, glistening in the torch light, a body, weeping, flesh fresh and oozing, a sickly smell in the hallway. It filled the room like fluid. The ... the thing ... stood there, staring down on Malik, weirdly perfect in its form, skinned naked, muscles showing, veins inching blood around its torso. Ligaments flexing.

Malik couldn't find breath for a moment, the words, "What the fuck," all but breathing from him. His hand snaked around behind him as he leant against the front door, reaching the door handle and twisting it.

Turning. Locked. *Still locked.*

"Even if I gave you the time to try to pick it again," the creature spoke, "you wouldn't be able to. Couldn't." Its red and wet features pulled to a smile. "Welcome to my home," it said.

"Who are you?" Malik breathed, his fingers still clenched on the door handle, white, blood not flowing to the muscles, tight. He couldn't believe his eyes. He had to be sick. That was it. Maybe this was a hallucination? Maybe he'd been drugged? What the fuck had Dance done?

Where was Dance?

"Does it matter?" the creature answered.

Malik raised an eyebrow in a moment of clarity. He supposed not, no. "What do you want?"

The creature took the handrail and slid its fingers down it as it descended the stairs, leaving a trail of smeared blood down the white painted wood. "A better question," it said. "You can let go of that now. It won't work."

Malik let the door handle go. It was surprisingly hard, to be honest. His fingers frozen in place. The way the creature talked, it was almost jovial. Light and breezy. Like visiting an uncle you'd hadn't seen for so long. That creepy uncle. The one who looked at you strange. An uncle with no skin. And, Malik could see being a little closer now, a wet, flaccid, penis.

The creature had no teeth, like it was malformed, or

even part formed. Something pulled from the sludge of a primordial soup, not yet what it would be.

"Are you going to tell me?" Malik was buying time to flee. He asked the question, his torch on the creature, but his eyes darting around. Left. Right. The girl. This explained the girl. This *thing* had done something to her. Whatever. No time for that shit. He could just charge a window. Hurl himself through. Before this thing had time to stop him. Fuck the police. Fuck getting caught. Nothing mattered apart from getting out. This thing was going to do to him what it did to her. And Dance.

"Where's Dance?" Malik asked.

There was a window in the living room, one that led straight out to the patio. That was probably the easiest one to go through. His eyes darted back to the creature. It was watching him. Studying him, perhaps.

"You want to leave?" it asked.

Malik nodded. "More than anything," he said. Which was very, very true. He hadn't said it loud though. Probably wasn't even the words he was looking for. It was just what his brain conjured at that second, but the creature heard it regardless.

"The one thing I cannot do," it said, returning the words no more loudly than Malik's own. And it did look remorseful. It looked like it wanted to let him leave more than it wanted anything.

But Malik still heard the words. "I won't say anything." Of course. Bargain with the creature. Let it know that you're not stupid enough to tell anyone what you'd seen, he thought. "I didn't see anything," he said.

"But you did," it responded with great sadness. "You have seen everything. You probably will see everything." It smiled at him. Like he should understand.

The creature nodded towards the living room and finished coming down the stairs. It went to the arch into the room, pausing only to say, "We should talk." It continued in, watched by Malik.

Fucking hell, he thought. He turned and rattled the door handle futilely, the door not budging. But that was okay. He pulled the picks from his pocket and crouched to work the lock. No lock. There was no fucking lock on the inside of the door. God ... *damn*. He scrunched his hands to fists and started smooshing them against his temples. Right. The window. He stood. Looked around. No way he was going to the living room and hurling himself out that window. Not with that thing in there. He flashed his torch around quickly, noticing the light in the living room going on. Window in the dining room. He turned running to the doorway. The window, there to the right of the bookcase. Old house. Old windows. Those ones that slide up and down. No wooden bars in the middle of the pane. Perfect. He started to run. Head down. He had to close his eyes before he hit the glass. Keep his hands up to protect himself.

The room was larger than he remembered, but that was good. More run up. As he got closer to the wall, he raised his elbows up. That was what he was going to use to smash through. Pray that he didn't shank himself on the splinters of jagged glass. Just as he launched. That last step. He noticed there was nothing outside the window. Nothing at all.

Just a vacuum of blackness.

He hit the window, smashing into it. Hard. Everything suddenly hurt. His arms felt like he'd been beaten with a bat, his head thumping. He couldn't see. Back hurt. He hit the ground with a thump and just lay there. The world swirling. But he was still breathing. That was something. He opened his eyes. Darkness. Ambient light. He drew air in his nose. A shadow circled his sight, getting closer in. Closing out ... everything. He was blacking out. *No*. He couldn't. He had to run. He pulled his eyes wider open and ... saw he was on the floor in the dining room. Hadn't gone through the window. Just bounced off.

"You can't leave," the creature said.

Malik looked up to it, standing in the doorway of the sitting-dining room. It flicked the light on and shook its head. Turning out.

"Do as you will. When you're ready, I'll be in the living room."

Malik pushed himself to his elbows, then up to sitting. What the fuck was going on? He got to his feet. It didn't feel right being in a room with the light on. He rolled out his arms and legs, tried to kick out the pain. Then he went to the door to the hallway. Couldn't get out the front door. Couldn't get out the window. He sighed. Didn't seem any point in going upstairs. The girl. The smell. He turned his torch off and pushed it back into his backpack. *Dance*, he thought. Where the hell was Dance?

Not that that seemed to matter now. Jeez. He went to the living room and looked around the corner, gingerly, like a scolded child at the head master's office. The creature was sitting in one of the chairs, in front of the fire. It was drinking a brown spirit out of a tumbler, a second glass and bottle on the table between the chair and a second chair. Malik blinked. The furniture had all been moved.

He was sure of it.

The room, long and thin, stretched away. Longer than it was before. "I don't understand," he said.

"You will," the creature responded. "Sort of." It turned in the chair and smiled back to Malik. "I barely understand it myself."

Malik shrugged his shoulders and continued down into the room. He went to the chair and sat. Looked at the creature. It left trails of viscera beneath its flesh as it sat there, teasing the rim of the glass with its forefinger. Unsure which way to look, Malik sucked in a lung full of air, and held it, looking around the now illuminated room. It was like before, but only *like*. Clearly the room was now longer than it had been. The number of chairs doubled, but more than that. There were items of objet d'art on the tops of the furniture. Things, the beauty of which he had never before seen. Items that he would have never forsaken had he seen them the first time he was in the room. They would have fit perfectly into his pack, and they were so utterly desirable. It was taking his entire will to not push himself from the chair and scoop up his pack from the floor, grabbing each and every one of them for himself. Dance would want them. But fuck Dance. Whatever happened to him. He realised the creature was studying him. His eyes returning to its.

"Have a drink," it said. Its eyes flickered to the

bottle on the table between them, the empty glass.

Malik looked at the smear of goo on the creature's own glass, and didn't want to go near anything it had touched, but looking, the bottle was clean. And he didn't want to seem rude. This was, after all, clearly some sort of demon, a monster. Something from a nether realm that had come here to punish him. Maybe he was dead? Him and Dance? Maybe they'd broken into the house and the owner was there, waiting for them. Farmer's shotgun. Blew their intestines halfway across the hall, guts flicking out, blood spatter redecorating the wallpaper.

"The fire is pleasant," it said.

Malik's eyes quickly searched the creature's skinless form. "I imagine," he said, without thinking. As soon as he'd said it, he realised.

But by then the two of them were staring at each other.

The creature started to laugh.

Malik watched its Adam's Apple bounce as a hearty roar slowed to a chuckle. A guffaw. Malik even drew a smile himself. Watching the creature find humour in its own ... predicament. He took the bottle up, looking quickly at the label. It was a scotch. A couple of centuries old according to the label, but Malik knew nothing of whiskey, nor had the ability to do the math required that quickly in his head to work out exactly how old the thing was. He pulled the cork. Wasn't used to a cork on a spirit. Usually a screw top. Maybe it was *really* old. He poured a half tumbler's worth into the glass and then pushed the cork back in. Corking a whiskey. It felt fancy. He put the bottle down, and took the glass, sniffing the liquid. It smelt smooth. Sweet, almost, like a Mac. Not what he was expecting. He thought it was going to be hard, harsh. Unpleasant. He watched the creature study the flames in the fire, composed now, the laugh seeming to break some of the tension. He sipped the whiskey. It was, truly, the finest whiskey he had ever had the pleasure of tasting. Never was one for it, but this? He felt like he could slowly sip this until the end of time, never boring of it, never wanting anything else. Literally, the best thing he had ever tasted. Tempted, as he was to pick up the bottle and note the label, he decided not to, simply because a) he could never afford something this old and this special, and b) he wasn't a good enough thief to be breaking into anywhere that had such an item. So he settled on taking another sip. He looked into the flames of the perfect fire, his look skirting back over the items in the room. The beauty. The luxury.

"It's a door," the creature suddenly said.

Malik just grunted. He wasn't really paying attention to the creature. He looked over to it. The comfort in the room, the cosiness, it was surrounding him, and he just didn't want it to stop. "What is?" he asked. His eyes were heavy. He felt like he was back in the womb, almost.

"You never asked the question, and you've been sitting there for far too long without speaking, so I guessed you had forgotten everything," it said.

Malik looked at it. "What?"

"I said you've been sitting there far—"

"I know what you said," Malik interjected, "I just want to know what you mean?" His eyes still on the fire. He guessed that was what his drinking companion was doing as well. Looking into the warmth of the fire.

"A door."

Malik finally turned his head and looked at the creature. "What is?" He sipped the liquid. His glass still half-full.

"The house."

It was interminable, trying to talk to someone like this. It was one of those difficult types, wasn't it? It was being ... obtuse. This time Malik took a larger mouthful of the beautiful liquid, rolling it around in his mouth, staring at the creature, still moist even under the heat of the fire. He was annoyed at its presence now. He swallowed the liquid, the burn more noticeable. "Tell me more, then," he said, sighing. Get this out the way. Then he could let the comfort of the room swallow him up again.

"The house," it said again. "It is the opening to something else."

"Something else?" Malik said without caring. He just wanted to get on with it.

"Something else," the creature echoed. "It is the beginning, and the end, and all things between."

"Uh-huh." Malik watched the flames licking up, sparks cracking. The gentle smell of smoke in the room.

"The house is the truth. And the truth will out."

"Riddles," Malik whispered. "You talk in riddles, my dear, skinless friend." He sipped the liquid, the soothing warmth. "Am I dead?" he asked.

The creature didn't respond, simply shaking its

head, perhaps disillusioned with the overwhelming incorrectness of the questions.

Malik looked at the thing. It was disgusting. Vile. A mess of flesh and gore. But it was, or at least used to be, human. "I don't understand."

"No," the creature replied. "That is because you won't ask the right questions and you certainly don't listen to the answers."

Malik stared at it as it placed its glass down and stood. The chair beneath, a mess of dried blood and pus, fluids wept into the materials over far too long. He blinked a few times. Tried to move the tiredness from his eyes. "Did I fall asleep?"

"Something like that. Come." The creature left the fire and walked slowly to the door. "It is time you saw more."

Malik pushed the glass carefully onto the table. He felt like he'd been drinking all night. His brain numb. Pushing himself to stand, he left his pack on the floor, too tired to pick it up. He just absently followed the creature to the arch into the hallway. The smell out there, different. Undoubtedly worse than it was earlier in the evening. Perhaps he had fallen asleep, maybe even several hours had gone by. "What are we doing?" he asked the creature.

The creature, already standing at the bottom of the stairs, turned back. "Come and see." It began up the stairs, the footprints it had left on them before, long dried.

The air in the house felt drier in Malik's throat. He followed, dutifully, with little choice it seemed. He looked up the stairs at the creature. It was all a little, dreamlike, to be honest. If Dance had something to do with this, he was going to pay for it. He stumbled on the steps, not lifting his foot quite as high as he should, it felt … heavy. Too heavy. His hand snapped out and landed on a step further up, holding his weight, and he was repulsed to see that his palm had landed in one of the creature's old footprints. He snatched it back, but the footprint simply dusted away. Malik looked back up to the creature, now standing on the first landing, watching. Waiting. "Coming," he said. Back to his feet he heaved himself up the stairs, feeling like a thousand pounds had been added. It had to be exhaustion. Maybe he was coming down with something. He rose, up the stairs, the creature leading, until they were back at the door of the bedroom.

The woman beyond.

The smell was unbearable now. Malik held his hand over his mouth, pinching his nose at the same time. "Jesus," he said. "What the fuck happened up here?"

"Time," the creature said. "Not always the great healer."

It pushed the door open, the heat from the room, decay, the stench of something decomposing. Malik stepped back, away from it, instinctually. But the creature stepped forward. Into the room. Beckoning Malik forward.

He was compelled. He had to know. So he followed. Into the room. His hand over his mouth. The room smelled worse ... clearly coming from the bed against the wall. He knew that it was the woman. Maybe she was dead now? Dance ... had Dance done something to her? Malik shook the thought away. No. He couldn't have. Wouldn't. He just wanted to turn the place over. His girlfriend. Partner. Whatever term he was using at the time. He thought too much of her. He did. He'd said so. What was her name? Malik still walked slowly to the bed, following the creature, absently trying to remember. The smell so strong he could taste it.

The creature waited. By the curtain. It held the material in its gloopy, sticky hands, until Malik was closer. Close enough. Then it pulled the curtain back. Just a little. Allowing Malik to see nothing but the woman's face.

Someone had clearly swapped the woman out for another. This woman that lay there now, old. Maybe in her sixties. She was breathing like the other. Her grey hair slicked back with sweat as she lay, undisturbed, a slight smile creeping onto her face, before disappearing just as quickly as it had come.

"What is this?" Malik asked.

"A door," the creature said.

Malik turned away, looking back into the room. There was a stereo in the corner. A bay, leading to a balcony. A way out for sure. He looked over at the post-modern wardrobes and then the other window. No TV. The bedroom should have a TV.

The creature dropped the curtain.

"You're playing with me," Malik said, matter of factly.

"No."

"Then why is everything changing?" He gestured wildly around the room, a moment of clarity in the bizarreness of the situation. The impossibility of it all. "It wasn't like this." He pointed to the bed. "She's not the same."

"She is not," the creature said. "But she is."

"Fucking riddles," Malik barked again. "Let me go."

"You cannot leave."

Malik's head spun. Forcing his way out hadn't worked before, but maybe this door, this balcony was different. Maybe he could get out that way. Although … he breathed, his shoulders, slumped. "Why has she changed?" he asked, quietly.

"Time has passed and she is older."

Malik shook his head. The words meant nothing because they couldn't be true. "Whatever. What's wrong with her?"

"There is nothing wrong with her."

"Then why is she like that? Comatose? But not. She shudders and shakes like she has a fever … is she sick?"

The creature dipped its head forward like it approved of what came from Malik's mouth. "Desire is subjective, and she chose poorly. It happens to everyone, eventually."

"What do you mean?" Malik shook his head. No. That wasn't good enough. "Explain to me what she has done, what did she choose that was poor?"

"She wanted to be pleased. Like everyone. And eventually she desired something that resulted in this— a rotten old woman, shuddering in pleasure constantly. Her body given out, dehydration ravaged, she feels like she is in the desert, there is a hunger within her that will never be sated, a thirst. Desire. Years without nourishment, and yet all the time she is rolling over the point of orgasm. Over. Over." The creature just stared at Malik while it spoke. "She is lost." It gained no pleasure in the words. It didn't seem to want what the woman had been given. The words relayed as nothing but fact.

"How long have I been here?" Malik asked eventually, his eyes resting on the creature.

"It is hard to tell, for me. I cannot answer that."

Malik looked at the woman, then the creature. He sucked in air through his nose, and then he turned away, the smell of rotten flesh, excrement.

Death.

He wanted to help her ... wanted to find Dance, but now he wanted to save himself. More than anything. "How can I leave?" he asked.

The creature didn't move, standing behind him the whole time. "You cannot."

"So what am I doing here?" An anger turned over in Malik. He wanted to spin on his heel and lash out at the creature. He wanted to ball his fists and throw them at the thing. He wanted ... the anger rose, and yet he pushed it back down. *The creature*, he thought. The creature. It was not of this earth. Perhaps brawling with it was not the smartest thing to do right now. He needed to be smarter. Not harder. He looked at the door out to the balcony. He could run at it. Right now. He could use his shoulder. That was what he should do. Run at the door and shoulder it open.

"You can have anything else," said the creature.

"Oh … fuck off," Malik whispered, absently. He looked at the door out to the hallway. Maybe he should check around the house before committing to throwing himself off a balcony. Back door. Basement? Something. He turned back to the bed.

The creature was gone.

"Huh," he said. "Hey. Where are you?"

The woman in the bed groaned out in ecstasy, making Malik shudder lightly. Right. He went to the bed and looked around the other side of it. The creature really was … *gone.* Rubbing the bridge of his nose, Malik went back to the door to the stairs. Maybe it was all a dream. That would have made sense. Because nothing else did.

He went downstairs and looked—room to room—for ways out. In every room the windows the same. A bleak, blackness beyond, and no matter what he tried, the glass was unbreakable. The back door, in the kitchen. When he saw it, he wasn't sure it had been there last time he was. Wasn't that where the sous vide machine had been? But regardless, the door had no lock. No windows.

The house, it appeared was sealed.

And it stank.

Malik sat at the dining table. He held a beer in his hand. He'd found it in the fridge. There was always beer in the fridge. No matter how many he took. Every time he opened the door. More beer. Good beer too. *Perfect* beer. He was tapping his nail on the can, pearls of condensation rising on the outside of it, dribbling down to the table beneath. His face resting in the cleft of his elbow as he watched it. "I must be dead." He didn't know how long he had been there.

There was no way of knowing.

He'd wanted to know. Sure. It was one of the things that he wanted to know after the creature had disappeared, and he'd even found a clock in the living room. Above where the fire used to be. That was where the TV was then. But it didn't make sense. Like none of this made sense. It didn't matter if he looked away from the clock for seconds, no more than a minute, when he looked back the time was different. It may as well have been a random number. When he'd lost his temper with it, stormed from the room, then changed his mind and returned, the clock was gone.

The house was fulfilling his every whim, that was for sure.

Except two.

The first was obvious. He couldn't leave. It wouldn't let him. And damn it, he wanted the creature back. He had questions now. Real questions. Questions that meant something, now he'd had time to think.

… but whatever. The second was the woman. She was rotting away, almost slower than time could perceive. She was on death's door when the creature showed her old, to him. How much time had passed since then? A week? A month? And still she lived. He'd pulled the sheets from her only last night. Her body was pocked with age spots, sores covering her. Her head almost bald. Cheeks thin. Yet still she came.

Shit.

He picked up the beer and tasted it. Perfect. He wanted so much. Things from the past, times and places that had been, and whenever he wanted enough, the house provided. A skewed representation of what he sought. He wanted food, it gave him food. Perfect food. But never the food he wanted. He craved chicken. It gave him perfect beef. He wanted to drink tequila, it gave him perfect beer.

He hated fucking beer.

He wanted company. A woman. A child. It had given him her. That was when he'd thought about fucking her. Maybe *that* was the way out of this purgatory. He thought for a while he was in Heaven. A place for him to live for eternity with nothing but his dreams fulfilled, but the solitude was overbearing. The loneliness. The smell of rotting flesh. The broken promises of dreams.

He pushed the can over, the beer chugging out to the table, pooling, then running off the edge, spattering on the floor. It also stank of puke in there. He'd drunk enough to kill a rhino a couple of times, hoping that it would end all of it. But all he'd done is pass out and woken up in the corner, covered in puke. He'd not bothered to clean it up. What was the point?

He looked around the dining room. Felt warm.

The room was too warm.

Malik pulled his shirt off. It stank anyway. He should wash it. Yet he discarded it to the floor. Went to where the library used to be. Sat in the single chair, pulling a porn mag from the shelving, the books, tens of thousands of pages of artistic expression and learning, replaced by piles of jazz mags. He flipped through the pages again. He'd read this one. Maybe. Maybe not. The pictures were different. The women, girls. Getting younger as the pages went by. Little more than teenagers. Younger. He closed the magazine and tossed it to the pile, toppling it. The magazines dropped to the ground, slowly, falling open as he watched, each one landing, flopping open on a new page, a naked body. All shapes and sizes.

It didn't matter to him.

He closed his eyes. Remembering who he was, before he'd ended here. Dance ... had Dance ended there? In his own Purgatory. This ... Hell?

The room still felt hotter. He looked at the windows. There were no coverings, and a sudden pang of self-consciousness fell over him. He wanted to remove his clothing, but ... the windows. He shook his head.

There was nothing outside the house. Nothing.

He stood. Pulled his clothes from his body, and stood naked. Looking down at the pictures in the magazines. Pictures of the past. The before.

He left the sitting room, going to the stairs and up. To the bedroom. The heat in there was oppressive, bringing with it a stench that he could only likened to a mass grave. Something the boys would have put together. Back in the day. He went to the bed and pulled the curtain across. The woman, what was left of her, still there. Naked. She was partially bereft of skin. Rotted away. Her lips had shrunken back, baring her yellow teeth, gaping holes where her gums receded and they had dropped from her. Blind, without the moisture to keep her eyes from working. She was beautiful, still, he thought.

If it would end it, he would lay with her. He swallowed, trying to breathe through his mouth. He pulled the sheet back, and looked at the piss and shit. He looked at her pussy, still wet. Climbing between her legs, he wanted to end it, and knew that this would. He didn't need to make himself hard.

The house did it for him.

And he lay with her, in filth.

———

It was perhaps a month later. A year. It felt like eternity. Malik lay there on the bed, next to her. He'd lost count of the times he'd consummated their togetherness, knowing that each time *had* to be the last. Until he'd awoken this time. Laying in the gut wrenching filth. She was dead.

Finally taken from him.

That *had* to be the end. He got from the bed, the first time he'd left the curtain in a millennia, padding naked and rotten across the room to the door. He looked out to the stairwell. "Why has nothing changed?" he shouted. "Why am I still here?" The words felt alien in his mouth, having said nothing but the mutterings of a mad man trying to ejaculate in a corpse for so long. He looked down at himself. Thin. Gaunt without food. His skin pallid and dry without hydration. He went downstairs. To the kitchen.

Pulled the fridge open, driven by thirst.

But it was empty. He tried the golden taps in the sink filled with garbage. They ran dry. "Fuck," he said, muttering. "Why?" He went back to the dining room. Closed his eyes as he stood there, light headed. Willing there to be a banquet on the table.

When he opened them, there was nothing.

He stumbled from the room. He went back to the hallway trampling the magazines that stayed there on the floor, fading with age. Across to the living room, where once there was a bottle of whiskey.

Where he found the creature, sitting in one of the chairs, facing the fire. There was a bottle of whiskey on the table between them, an empty glass. Malik went to the chair. "Nice of you to join me," he said. He slumped down. The sores on his body splitting open, pus flowing out. He ignored the burning sensations. And the glass. He grabbed the bottle by the neck and spun the lid off. Taking a gulp. The cheap, harsh liquid, burning his throat, easing the pain of dehydration none. "Bollocks," he said, trying not to spit it out, swallowing the saliva it produced, trying to calm his belly, suddenly rancid and turning. Sickness and bile in his throat. "Am I dead?" he asked.

"We all are," said the creature.

"Is this Hell?"

"Almost," the creature said. "The house is a door."

Angry, Malik took another swig of the burning

liquid, ignoring the discomfort of consumption. The acrid taste of blood in his mouth. "Why are you doing this to me?"

"*I* am doing nothing to you," the creature said. Focussing its look on the flames in the fireplace.

"What happened to me?"

"Dance killed you."

Malik took a deep breath. "What?" The word slipped from him, without thought, just as the answer made the anger slip from him. A sudden calm over coming him.

"Dance killed you," the creature echoed.

"How … why?"

"He bludgeoned you to death, because you raped his sister."

Malik sat back in the chair a little. He hadn't realised that Dance knew about that. Raped was a strong word. "Oh," he said. That was all that came out. "It was business," he said. He had a sudden urge to justify his actions to the creature.

"I know. It always was, with you. Wasn't it? Just a cog in the machine."

"Yeah." He was. An actor in a movie. He wasn't doing anything truly wrong. Was he? "So why am I here?"

"Because you raped children. Robbed. Murdered. Thieved. I'm sure someone else will go through the details with you."

Fuck. The whiskey rolled in Malik's stomach. A

door. Malik knew where the door led now. Not somewhere he'd ever believed in. But it looked like it was all true. He glanced to the window. Maybe he could still get out. Maybe. Maybe it wasn't too late. That was it. It was like that Dickens novel. This was all just showing him the way. Giving him a chance to right his wrongs. Repent. He pushed himself to his feet. Wobbly, yet somehow relieved. He stepped back, behind the chair. The creature didn't bother to move. It just watched the fire. The room hotter than ever before.

That was why it had returned, wasn't it? It was time. Time to cross over. Go through the door.

Well, fuck that.

Malik still held the whiskey. He took one last swig, the liquid slippery in his mouth, coppery, mixed with the blood. He lifted it like a bludgeon and brought it down, as hard as his atrophied body would allow, onto the back of the creature's head. Both their skulls caving in. A sharp hard pain in Malik's head, followed by a serene numbness, he stumbled forward, dropping the bottle. Holding onto the back of the chair, the creature … gone. He felt sick for a moment. Blood in his mouth. He turned and looked at Dance, just for a moment, before collapsing to the floor. Brain matter flowing from his skull, as he stared, dead eyed to the fireplace and the flames of Hell.

HATCHING

ONE

THE CRACKLE OF BURNING FIRE.

She was pregnant, right?

Right.

And there were these lesions on her. Down there.

And you'd know that … how?

"It happens."

"It happens."

"Shut the fuck up. It *does*. So anyway. She's having a rough time of it. She's huge. I mean fucking huge. Like there are two or three sprogs in there. She's got this scabby skin going on. Like pus and ooze all over the place. Almost like she's rotting from the inside. So she goes to the quack and the guy does an examination and he tells her that there's nothing to worry about."

I mean, why would there be? It's just some skin irritation that she's not been looking after. Gotten raw and such. So, he gives her a prescription for some cream—steroid or some shit—and sends her on her way. Scripts are fucking expensive these days, right? Nearly ten quid. Anyways, she takes the script, goes down to the chemist. There's one in the car park of the doctors, of course. She goes in and gets it filled. Goes home.

Nothing to worry about. Skin infection. Got cream. Kid weighs a fucking ton, but the doc seems fine with it and so why should she worry? She thinks she's big, but she's seven months in. Had a scan a few weeks ago and they said everything was fine. So, she goes home, and undresses.

Gets herself buck fucking naked. Looks at herself in the mirror. She can see the scabs that way, easier, you know? Being friggin' preg. She looks down her body. Doesn't like it much. There's discolouration on the skin from stretch marks and she's thinking that she'll never be the same. She was hot. She knew it. Men fawning all over her. But she doesn't care about that. She *liked* being hot. Autosexual. Fucked herself in the mirror. Sometimes better than the dudes she could pick up so easily in the bar could, that was for sure. But anyway. She's not finding herself so attractive now. But … she *has* got to fix this skin problem. She knows that. And she doesn't have anyone to help. Hasn't had anyone near her since the day she found out she was pregnant. She stopped going out. Everything. Hasn't even had a drink. Her mum told her not to have the kid alone, but she was sure. She wanted it.

When she looks in the mirror, she's not so sure now, though. Is she?

She sits on the edge of the bed. Her belly pushes out and she can barely see her knees. That's why she has to do it in the mirror. She squirts some of this cream on her fingers and she tries to reach around the lump. She gets it smeared in places, mapping herself around her body in the mirror, it's all backwards, ain't it? But she tenderly gets the cream on her fingers close to the skin on her thigh. She can see it there, and as she moves she can feel the peaks on the cream teasing her flesh. Tingling. Tickling. She feels it in the right place. Looks right in the mirror, and then she pushes her fingers against the sores.

First, there's a burning sensation, but that eases as she smooshes the stuff about. The burning transforms to a cooling as she continues to rub, closing her eyes, the pain subsiding and relief taking over.

Her breathing increases in speed, her body taking a sigh in pleasure. She takes her hand from her thigh and brings it to her face, grabbing the tube of cream, wanting more of the relief, the pleasure that the cream gives. It trickles through the body, and tingles every part with nothing more than just the removal of the itching and the pain, and the …

She looks at the mess on her fingers. Yellow pus smooshed into the white cream. Flecks of blood from the broken skin. She looks up from the hand to the mirror and can see her leaking a mixture of colours to the bedsheets. She gets up, hurries to the bathroom and washes the putrid mess of what looks like bolognaise sauce from her hand. Weeps slightly at the realisation that her beautiful skin is horribly blemished and there is nothing she can do about it because she can't reach it, and fuck going to the hospital for a rash that the doc has told her is absolutely fine and there is nothing to worry about.

She blubs out a cry, as tears flop onto her face and she leans down, two hands firmly on the sink and looks up, into the bathroom mirror. There are streaks of mascara on her face, where she put the cheap stuff on to go to the doctor. She should have put on the waterproof, apparently. Now she looks like a shit horror movie cover. She sucks snot back into her nose, as she breathes swallowing it down into her throat like cold cum, and she straightens.

Doc said it would be okay. So it's okay.

She goes back to the bed and starts again. Admiring her perfect breasts in the mirror. Taking solace that there is nothing wrong with her or the child. It's just a skin sore and hormones. That's all it is.

I wish I didn't have a child. I wish I'd never gotten pregnant, she thinks.

"Push," the older woman orders.

She's long forgotten her name. She shouldn't be there. She should never have been there. Eight months in and she decided to take a weekend break in Wales on her own. Then, while she's in the countries largest second hand bookshop, her waters break. She didn't even realise at first. TV always lies, though doesn't it? She was expecting some splashing or gushing or some shit. Now she realises that it's thicker. Like a translucent porridge. A goo, like they'd drop on Pat Sharp's kid's shows on Saturday morning. Stinks too. Like rotting meat, with a hint of honey in the mixture. The shit slops down her leg while she's got some hardcore BDSM erotica in her hand. She *was* going to buy it too, after she's checked the pages, of course, because *second hand porn*, but then some kid screamed and pointed and she looked down to find this mess of xenomorph spit dropping out of her preggo dress and pooling on the ratty carpet beneath her. She screamed. The kid continued screaming, and then some old woman got faint and had to hold herself up. To be honest, she had expected more people to be aware of the intricacies of birthing.

So, the assistant had run over and taken her hand and called an ambulance.

"*Push*," the woman barks.

And now she's here, *pushing*. Looking up into the poor, flickering lights of some rando NHS hospital. Fuck. She's in Wales. Is it still the NHS? She's not getting charged for this shit, is she? Her head flops back. Another woman leans over her. Eyes in hers. "Come on," she says. *One last time.*

So she pushes, one last time.

There's a sudden jar in her. And she can feel the weight shift. Something has certainly happened. There's a split second of silence, and then a scream fills the room. She doesn't know who. She just knows it's not her. A crash. Something falling. She leans up. There's a sudden sense of dread and fear. There must be something wrong. *Not the baby, not the baby.* She says it in her head over and over like a mantra. She lifts her head. Legs up in stirrups. She looks over the bump and sees the darkness coming over it. Like a horde crashing over a hill.

A thousand baby spiders crawling all over her … from where the baby was. *Is*. Air catches in her throat and she stares at it for nothing more than a second, and then the same scream that filled the bookshop, the same scream that fills the birthing room … it comes from her. Instinct is to move. She yanks her left leg from the stirrup, not strapped in or anything, and she tries to roll, from the chair/bed/gurney thing she's paid no attention to, bapping down at herself, trying to get the fucking things from her.

She doesn't realise that they aren't just on her. They're coming *from* her.

Falling from the bed, she lands on the hard floor of the hospital room on her hands and knees. Screams out in pain, looks down at herself, under herself. Her belly resting on the floor. The baby. It's still inside her, but she's crawling in fucking spiders. "Get them off of me," she screams. She can feel them over her, her legs, her vagina running in them, she can feel them scurrying over her like ants on a hill. The dawning of them coming from inside, the goo from the bookshop. The rash on her legs. Spiders digging beneath the flesh.

She rolls over, brings her knees up. She pushes. There is a squirt of slime that fires from her over the bleached floor of the room. The hospital staff have all fled. To the corners of the room. Pushed up against it, trying to push *through* it. All painted with looks of horror. She pushes again, and the gelatinous fabric of what was once a child drops from her, covered in jelly, like a chicken in a can, and the thousands of them descend upon it, lunch being served.

"Boring." Daniel scuttles across the log he sits on to Steve's side. "Heard it before."

Steve shakes his head. "No fucking way. It only happened last week." He glances into the darkness that surrounds the fire they've made. It's gotten dark since he started the story. His eyes rest on Jo. Her face is gurned into some horrific stare. Mouth pulled back.

Eyes wide. He starts to laugh at her.

Then Daniel joins in. "What?" he says. "You can't be bothered by *that* bullshit. The one about the dude in the backseat of the car at the petrol station was scarier than that one, and we've heard it all a million times." He looks to Steve. "What's with her?"

Jo shakes her head, finally moving. "You don't understand," she says.

"Not preggo are you?" Steve asks.

"No." She pulls the blanket that was covering her knees up a little. Over her torso, her shoulders. Eyeballs the marshmallows in the pack, and the leftover burger meat, limp and browning on the ground.

"Fucking hell, it's just a story."

"You don't understand." Her fingers drop instinctively to her lap for protection.

Steve sighs. "I'm sorry. It *was* just a story."

Jo looks to the fire, distraught, and then back over her shoulder to the two tents behind them. Daniel snorts. "It's not real. There are no spiders in this country that'll lay eggs inside you."

"None," Steve says. "Look, have this." He pulls a joint from his pocket, stumpy one, and hands it forward. Jo takes it and lights it. She doesn't hand it back after having a couple of drags. Rude. But Steve lets her off this time. You know. The story. And the other thing. He takes a small plastic bag from his pocket. Dips his damped finger into the crushed black powder and then sucks it off like he's sucking sherbet. Or Daniel. Smiles to himself at the thought, then hands the bag to Daniel. "So what's happening going forward?" he says. Tries to keep the tone down. Bit more serious.

"Jared said that when I get back on Monday, he'll stay out the flat for a couple of days for me to collect my shit together and get out. He's being pretty decent about it." She visibly relaxes as she blows the smoke out over her head. "Are you sure it's going to be okay if I stay with you two for a week or two? Just to get my shit together?"

She's already asked. Like, a hundred times. "Of course," says Daniel.

Steve gives him a glance, but he's already dipping into the mushroom powder for a second hit. "Christ," he whispers, his eyes back on her. "As long as you want. We've got the space."

"And we know how to party," adds on Daniel. He starts giggling. The first lot of mushrooms taking a hold. He'll be uncontrollable once the second lot kicks in.

Jo looks around the ground. She leans forward to the leftovers and pulls the knife that Daniel had speared into the dirt. Drops it down behind the stump she's sitting on. Best not to have knives sitting around when you're all tripping. "Party hardy," she says, returning her look to the two of them. "Nerds." The two men look at each other quickly and smile before Steve takes the baggie back and goes for a second dip. "Leave some of that for me," Jo says. Everything was going to be fine with those boys.

She'd known them for years. She trusted them when they told her things like that.

TWO

A CRACK IN THE DARKNESS

Jo opens her eyes. The blackness is all-encompassing in the tent. The trees create a canopy over the clearing and the moon doesn't get through. Barely a glint, and that is certainly not visible from inside. She turns on the self-inflating stupid thing she is supposed to sleep on and grumbles a little, before turning back again and staring into the blackness.

She can't hear anything. The boys must have turned in.

Thank God.

That's the last thing she needs to hear. Them at it. She's heard them before. Once or twice and they're noisy fucks. All groans and moans and *yes's* and *fuck me's*. She takes a long sigh. The air going in, she holds it. Waits. Shit. She needs to remember to breathe out. The air escapes and she lets her blow of air turn into a giggle. Fucking shrooms.

Noises. She focuses on them. Outside the tent, the forest moves in a strange and delightful way. The darkness, a cover for all sorts of malarkey.

Then the crack of a twig. Her first thought. Bears. Then she remembers that unlike all the Youtube camping videos from Canada, there are no bears there. Only spiders. She continues to stare into the nothing. Non-poisonous spiders. So there isn't anything to worry about. And, she checked the tent before she got in. Fucking Steve and his fucking stories. She turned the whole lot out. She doesn't remember the ins and outs of it though. She was a bit wasted by then. Feeling a little better now. But she clearly remembers making the boys pull everything out the tent and making sure there was nothing in there. She closes her eyes and remembers the sleeping bag, discarded to the ground while they looked. What if a spider got in the sleeping bag? What if there is one in there with her now? Her heartrate rises. Blood pumps quicker around her veins.

It's okay, she tells herself. Even if there was a spider in there with her

—which there isn't

then it's not poisonous. Is it? She turns again, pushing her head into the pillow. Feels something move in her hair and reaches out quickly and brushes it. Nothing. She can't see anything. There could be spiders crawling all over her and she wouldn't know.

It was just a hair.

She sighs. Another deep breath. Fuck it. Fuckers. Fucking campfire horror stories. Balls. Right. She sits. Fingers into the hair, running it through like scissors and pulling them out, closed, brushing anything that might be in there, out.

Nothing. She doesn't think. But there could be. She fumbles around the side of the sleeping bag and finds her phone. The luminescence of the screen warms her, but she flips the torch on anyway, shining it around the interior of the tent.

See. Nothing. She knew there was going to be nothing. See. She knew.

She flops back down on the inflatable and stares into her phone for a moment. There is a message from Jared. He sent it a while ago, but long after dark. Laying in bed alone. Fucker's got horny. Hate that word. Sounds like a teenager thing. Dirty and cheap. Like him. Her thumb over the message, thinking about opening it. Her brain is telling her it's probably a cock pic and a message telling her he's waiting at home. All is forgiven. Wanting a leg over. But he wasn't the one to do the forgiving ... was he?

Her thumb flicks the phone off and she drops it down the side of the mattress. *Bastard.* The blackness has taken back over. And she closes her eyes.

Maybe try and sleep some more.

———

There is a sudden burning pain. Jo opens her eyes. Even though she knows they're wide, she can't see shit. "Fuck," she whispers out, her hand instinctively going down, into the sleeping bag and to the site of the pain. She probes the spot, on her thigh, feels for the cause. Then she thinks it's the spider.

The one that came in from when the sleeping bag was outside. She pushes herself backwards, hard, tossing herself from the inflatable mattress onto the base of the tent. She feels her phone going underneath her as she kicks herself over the top of it. Out. Into the tent. Fingers on the wound. She grabs at the phone and thumbs at it, panicked. "Fuck," she grunts. Louder this time.

Pain in her leg when she probes the bite. "Fuck." Again, louder. She pulls her hand from the waistline of her sweat pants. The light from the torch flicks on. The tent lit. She pulls her foot from the sleeping bag and pulls herself tight into a ball, one hand on the torch, the other around her legs, pulling them into her chest. Eyes on the sleeping bag. Waiting to see the thing that just bit her. The monster.

Creature.

It did bite her, right? She thinks about the spider, laying eggs in her. "No," she says. "No, no, *no*." Jo scrabbles to the edge of the tent and fumbles to grip the zip, pulling it down from the roof of the canvas, to the ground, her fingers touching the grass beyond, sending a shiver up her arm as the feeling reminds her of insect legs grabbing at her as she tries to flee. She withdraws. Afraid to leave the safety of the tent. Then her look flicks to the sleeping bag and the thing that is in there, her look, determined, goes to the flap of the door, and then she pushes away. Out to the safety of the forest.

Bare feet in the darkness, on the damp of the grass, the leaves shed from the trees. Dirt. She stumbles out into the night, and turns. Torch on the tent. Like this creature might be chasing her. Not a spider, laying eggs in her.

She looks down to herself. Shit. Yes. The bite. The laying. Whatever. She starts to pull at her joggers. No use, trying to pull them down with one hand, so she discards the phone to the leaves, the light emitting from it, spinning around the dark like a rave light. Both hands on her sweats, she pulls them down to her knee and her fingers probe to the bite. The wound. Whatever. Red, it already looks like a boil in the dim light of the phone dancing in the forest, the shards of moonlight cutting through the perfect black.

"Fucker," she says. Touches the bump. Splinters of pain spear through her as she does. She hisses air in. The pain burns like a candle flame touching her skin. "Balls," she says. The blackness around her increasing the feeling. She turns. Shambles forward with her trou around her ankles like a fucking baby. Closer to the fire. The light. The glow of the fire turns her skin a hue of orange. Bending forward she looks at the lump. In the light of the fire it's redder. Burnt orange. "Boys," she hisses into the night. "Fucking help me." She turns to their tent. Stares into the darkness.

Left. Then right.

Where the fuck … the thought slips off into the recesses of her brain. Cunts. They've packed up and left. "Steve, you bell-end," she shouts into the forest. "This isn't a joke."

The sound of the nothing enveloping her replies, with little more than the rustle of trees and movement beyond her field of vision. Animals moving in the night. Jo realises she's shaking. Sweating, too. She's too close to the fire. The heat on her skin drying it. Beads of sweat trickling into the heat spot and burning away. "Daniel. *Daniel?*" She turns, her shadow pirouetting around her like a troupe of ballet dancer's swishing to and fro the stage of Swan Lake. Eyes unable to focus on the shadows as they move.

They're not there. They're not *fucking* there.

"You bastards," she screams into the night. "You *fucking* bastards."

She turns, again, and again. They weren't there. This wasn't a fucking joke. They've fucked off and left her in the middle of the fucking forest. She stops. Thinks. She has no idea where she is. How to get back to the car. The fucking car. That would be gone too.

A moment of forgetfulness, and then there is a stabbing pain in her leg again. She looks down at the bite. "Fuck you," she mutters. She stops. Looks at her discarded phone. That would do it. She takes a single step forward.

And that was when the thing in her leg moved.

THREE

FROM THE MOUTH OF BABES

Jo screams out in agony as the thing under her skin moves. It feels like it is clawing through her flesh, trying to dig deeper like a bargain hunter at a jumble sale. She doesn't think. Puts her foot down normally and the weight is too much, it gives, and she tumbles to the ground. Screaming out in pain, fear. New pain spikes up her shoulder as she lands, crook. Pain overcome with numbness. Her immediate thought is that it is poison. She was being fucking poisoned. She rolls onto her back. Takes stock, quickly. Everything else moves normally. Shit. She is fine. It was the fall.

Then pain from her leg again. Burning into the thigh. Up, around her hips. She moans, deep guttural sounds coming from her, before they morph into this screech.

"Fuck you, fuckers." She launches the words out into the forest, aimed squarely at the boys, gone, part of the practical joke. She pushes herself up onto haunches and looks down to the bare skin. The purple bruising around the site of the bite, the lump there, under the surface, moving like she's never seen before. It's digging around, trying to lift the dermis from the flesh, to scuttle about under her skin like a cat in a bed, covered and warm. Bloody and sticky. She looks around the ground. The empty site. There's nothing. Just the fire, and her tent. Pushing to get herself up, the pain overcomes her and she slumps back down onto her arse. Rolls quickly to the side and gets on her hands and knees and crawls towards the fire.

She has to get this thing, or these *things*, from her. Before she becomes a campfire tale herself. Every time the leg goes down the pain rises, but she ignores it and moves forward. The heat of the fire burning to her face as she gets close. She stops close to the roaring flame. Breathing hard. Sweat beating its way down her face making her damp and gummy. The air muggy. Staring into the flame, entranced for a moment, she cries out a blub, a sob, as she searches the base of it.

There. In the tent of branches and twigs that Steve used to create the opening flame she sees the long hard stick, pointed, burning hot. But sticking out far enough for her to grab. To reach. She hisses as the flames lick her knuckles as she grabs at it. A spear of wood. Pulling it from the fire, she rolls away, the heat on her face too much. Before she stops next to the campfire. On her back. Air sucking in and out. Then up on one elbow. She looks at her leg. The lump is gone. No. It managed it. It managed to move. Fuck. She rolls, trying to see more. There it is. One second on the back of her leg as she twists impossibly like a yoga guru. It moves. Back around the front. She moves with it, dancing macabre in the glow of the flames in the darkness of the night, just to keep eyes on the intruder in her body. Every move births new pain inside her, aches and burns from the muscle movement, stabs and cuts from the interloper.

It stops.

She eyes it for no more than a split second. Then raises the weapon she still grips and stabs it into the flesh. Into the boil. Throbbing and burning. The spider moves at an alarming rate. Away. Out of the way. It's gone and all she achieves is stabbing herself in the leg. Deep with a dirty spear. She screams again. "*No.*" Crying out in pain. Frustration. The creature moving fast in the network of caves inside her leg. She closes her eyes and begs it doesn't get inside her deeper.

Please, she prays. Stay on the surface.

She pulls the spear from her leg. Blood oozing from the end of it. Dark and deep in the night. Her leg a gouged mess of flesh, the stick digging flesh out from her. She feels the burn of the pain as it rises before it becomes the new feeling.

A river of hate and bile, acid burns and crawling monsters finds its way up her nerve endings to her brain and then it stops her. Paralysed by the pain she slumps back. The intruder momentarily forgotten. She rolls to her back. Looks through the canopy of trees to the night sky above. Cool and inviting. She wants to roll in something cold. Take the burning from her. Then she breathes in fast and deep like she'd forgotten how to.

Sits.

She looks at her leg and the blood gooing and gushing from the prick wound. The small spear not pulled back out straight, levering the flesh from the muscles and the tendons and the bone. Her fault. Not the creature. She pulls the baggy t-shirt she wears from her torso and tears a section from the waist. Moments pass as she sits there, nearly naked in her panties and trou, dropped around her knees. Bare from the waist up.

Wrapping a torn rag from the shirt around the gape in her leg. She ties it tight. Like she's seen on TV. Stem the flow of blood.

Before the memory of the interloper returns.

Suddenly naked in the forest, she pulls the remnant of the shirt back over her head and grabs up the stick. Looking around the tourniquet on her leg. It has to be there somewhere. She holds the spear. The pain taking all other feeling. She can't feel the creatures movement now.

Then it's there. Upper leg. She cries out seeing it move. It's coming for her groin. It's looking for the torso. She can't stop it where she's fleshier. She stabs down into the leg. Thinking. Not at the spider. At where the spider *will be*. A few inches in front of it. Ahead of the game. Like a video game. Shoot at where the space invaders *will be*.

Like a sacrificial dagger held over a virgin, Jo plunges the stick into her leg. Deep. Into the site of where the spider will be. The two of them become one. The lump, moving under the skin. Pierced perfectly by the stick. She feels it go through the skin. Popping her like there was air beneath. Into the flesh below and down, tearing muscle, until it hits the bone. The pain becomes unbearable. She slumps back, onto her back and looks into the coolness of the sky again.

Raging flares of agony exploding like fireworks in her leg. She stops for a moment, waiting for it to subside, satisfied that the creature is gone, and she only has to deal with her own fucked leg now.

The pain, easing, making the feeling of blood running from the stab wound, the stick still deep inside her, makes her move. Pushing herself up, supported by her hands, just behind her. She looks at the spear, sticking from her leg. Blood slowly fighting from the edges of it. She weeps, barely able to control the pain, she wants to curl into a ball and die. But she can't. The fuckers have left her to stay there alone and what ... wait for morning when they'll jump out on her and surprise her?

Jokes on them if she's bled to death.

Her breaths come and go stuttering from her. Unable to stop the tears flooding down her cheeks. She looks at the wood. Knows what she has to do. The wound just above the other. She pulls the shirt from her head and holds it there. Wondering the best way to tackle this. *Like before*, she tells herself. *Try to think straight*. She tears another strip from the shirt, turning it into a tube top and pulls the last of it over her head, barely covering enough to make her decent. Then she holds the rag in one hand and the stick in the other. She slows her breathing to a stop and then pulls. As straight as she can this time. The stick yanking from her flesh. The blood geysers up and out like a hose before stemming down to a drool. She pushes the shirt rag down to the blood, hard. This ring of blackness surrounding her vision. Jo fights, blinking the black back to the edges of her periphery. She knows that if she blacks out she'll die from blood loss. At least, that is what *she thinks* she knows. Maybe in real life if you black out, you just wake up again. No real blood loss.

"Shit." *It's the blood loss* talking, she thinks. "Fuck." She pulls the rag from the wound with the intention of wrapping it back around like the other.

But she stops and looks into the cave in her leg.

Full of yellow pus and stinking like a dead hedgehog. "Fuck," she snaps, holding her hand over her nose. It has to be the spider ... corpse. Fuck. She shouldn't leave that in there, should she?

But what choice does she have? She looks at the tent. The fire. There's literally nothing here to help her with that. Looking at the rag, she decides to wrap it. Fuck it. She'll get an infection, but she can probably get to a hospital tomorrow. She looks over to the phone, still laying in the dirt on the other side of what used to be the camp. *Of course.*

She starts to get to her knees. The pain riding her, legs to her back. Up to her neck. Her head. Throbbing like she hasn't had a drink of water in days.

She crawls slowly across the dirt to the phone. Blood and pus and shit oozing from her leg. As she crawls her joggers scooping crap from the ground making it harder. She reaches the phone and grabs it. The battery is fine. But she switches the torch off. Looks at the thing. No signal.

That doesn't matter though, right?

Emergency calls go through anyway. Don't they? Shit. Is that just an urban legend? Fuck it. *Just try.*

Then the feeling of a melon being pushed through the wound in her leg begins and she cries out. The phone forgotten for a second, she looks past it to the thing crawling from the pus. The thick mucus yellow liquid splitting as a leg from a spider the size of her hand pierces it and slides, slips, out, to the skin, using it to lever more legs out.

She births the arachnid while she stays, watching, frozen in fear. The long slender legs of a daddy long, then pulling out the body. The fat of its back as big as her palm. It extricates itself from her flesh. Before standing there. The two of them seemingly looking at each other. Eyes to eyes. Before it crawls around the side of her leg and steps gracefully to the ground. Between her legs. Yellow sticky liquid stringing the two of them together, holding the insect between her legs. Warm goo. Mozzarella. Cum.

She remembers to breathe. Just quickly.

Then the thing scurries away into the shadows. Away from the fire. Into the trees behind the tent.

Her heart hammers in her chest. The blackness around her vision dancing a tango, quickly. Mamba, maybe. The sound of drums filling her head. She can't black out. She knows she *can't*.

Oh, but you can, says a voice somewhere in the dark recesses of her soul.

Oh, but you can.

FOUR

CHILDREN ARE A GIFT

Jo jerks awake. Her eyes firm on the sky above. The black silhouette of the trees swaying gently from side to side. She blinks a few times. The memories of it all returning. She remembers the pain before she feels it. The cold of the night, her near naked body. Cold and numb. She rolls to the side. Her phone there in the dirt next to her. She reaches up and grabs it.

She's still alive. That's something.

The pain in her leg is agonising. She pushes herself up and touches the screen on the phone. Nothing.

No. It was fine. When? How long was she out? Fuck. It's still dark. It couldn't have been that long, could it? She holds the power button. Maybe it just powered off? Maybe. The load screen comes up, just for a split second and then goes. Back to dead.

"No," she whispers. "You have to be shitting me." She feels sick. Puke rattling around inside her. She pushes herself up. Looks at her leg. No blood, but that sticky pus shit is still everywhere. Leaking out of her. The smell of the dead. Rotting. She turns her head and puke dribbles over the dead leaves piled next to her. Notices the fire is burning still. Christ. The acid from her stomach rises more, the inside of her throat flayed as she wretches again. Tastes it on her teeth. "When I get home, I'm going to kill the pair of you," she mutters.

Jo pushes herself around onto her hands and knees and crawls towards the tree line. She feels in the leaves and dirt, looking for a branch or something that she can use as a crutch. She's going to have to walk out of here, isn't she?

The leg throbs.

She twists and picks up the rag from beside her, ties it around her leg. The feeling of the material on the wound is like acid sandpaper, eating away at her flesh, infected and rancid. She goes back to crawling. Looks back towards the fire. The phone discarded and left behind. She gets nearer the trees.

The trees where that fucking spider that climbed from her disappeared to. Aware, suddenly that it could still be there, watching her. She's hesitant. Full of fear. She stops everything. Staring into the darkness.

Noises that have always been there, slowly turning around her. *What if it's the spider?* She thinks. Trembling. On her hands and knees. She scours the forest floor for something … anything … to help get her back to her feet.

A branch. It'll do. She scrabbles to it. Grips it in her hand tightly and brings it to her chest. Maybe she's trembling because she's cold. Perhaps. Scared. She looks around the dark, then down to her leg. The pus drooling from beneath the bandage. She uses the branch like a walking stick and pushes herself up, keeping the weight from the leg and manages to stand, hobbling to the nearest tree and leaning against it.

What if the thing's above me? she thinks. What if it's there, waiting in the tree to jump down upon her? Biting her again. Impregnating her with another child like the last. She pushes from the tree, tottering and falling to the dirt, causing more pain to jig on her body like the lower decks of a ship, the drunk hands dancing and jiving all over her. She wails out in pain, but worse, her desire to keep going flails about. She just wants to stop. She just wants to be at home in bed.

Then a movement stops her sobs and her cries and wails. In the darkness, something moves.

Something huge.

———

Jo screams in the next tent. Daniel turns over, his hand sliding over Steve's torso. "What the fuck was that?" he asks.

Steve just shrugs, his eyes wide open. "She should have never mixed and matched the alcohol and the weed and the mushrooms. Probably a bad trip."

———

Jo stops moving. She looks into the darkness. And there. She can see it. Eight long legs, as big as she is. As tall as she. The thorax of the spider as big as a car, and as it stands there and watches her, she feels it … knowing it's the one she birthed. "Please God," she says.

"There is no God," the spider replies. "Only I."

Jo backs away from the thing, crawling like a

spider herself on the dirt, belly up, hands down. Backing away, away towards the fire. "What are you?" she screams. Fear filling her every orifice.

"Don't you recognise me?" it says. The words coming from somewhere beneath its torso, some unseen, impossible mouth, the words oozing out, deep and full of base. It snorts. "I am your offspring. Birthed of your flesh."

Jo scoots back on the dirt, across the floor, further, twisting as she moves, turning so she can get up. Ignoring the pain of the wounds on her legs, this wretched stabbing all the time as she bends her knees and takes weight on it. Uses the walking stick to push herself up to stand.

She faces the spider as it steps out from the shadows. Legs creasing at weird and unnatural angles as it brings first one up, then the next, out into the opening. The light of the moon luminescent on its back. Shimmering like a pond in the night. She continues away, back, passing the fire. Coming to a stop at the stump she was sitting on earlier. Time so long ago, it feels.

The creature stepping out into the light, its form there, the light from the fire hueing its underbelly a warm vermilion, the moon stark with a light blue on top. It chirrups and chirps as it stands before her. Front two legs up, moving slowly at first and then juddering with a light quickness. Jo jumps when it moves like that, like she is the prey and not the mother. "What do you want?" she whispers.

"I want what we all want upon birth. I am afraid. I want to return to the womb."

Jo glances down herself. To her legs, secreting infectious slime from the second wound. The place of birthing. Torn open. Blood mixing with the yellow snot. Fluid because of the motion and movement. Pulling the light scabbage open under the rag of her half-shirt. Leaking from her once again. "Leave me alone," she says.

"I want to come home." The legs that were up, come down to the dirt, spearing with strength into the leaves, piercing the earth. The other legs, pulled forward, motion, momentum. It moves at her and she stumbles.

She falls backwards over the stump and crashes in to the dirt. Sprawled. The walking stick gone from her sight. The stump between her and the fire and the light. The darkness surrounds her, the spider looming. Coming closer.

Jo's hand feels around the darkness, trying to find the stick to help her stand, her fingers finding something, she wraps them around it, and pulls it towards her. Not the walking stick, but *a* stick. She waves it at the creature. It's shorter, but broken off into a sharp point. The spider, the child, *her* child right there, the fire behind it, up on its back legs, reared like a horse.

Backlit, the spider looks like an effigy at a festival. A thousand people surrounding it, chanting fills the air. Jo can do little, but watch as the spider is worshipped in the night. Dancing around the fire, becomes dancing around the spider. Two legs buried in the dirt, the others raised up like a shaman, calling for the Gods to come forward, but it is the God. The light surrounding it. The worshippers fall to their knees and drop forward in prayer. In servitude. The chants becoming little more than a hum in the night. Jo is sweating out a fever. The infection is rampant in her system. Mind, confused. She doesn't remember how she got there. She doesn't remember how she can get back. She just knows that she needs a hospital.

And that she has to kill the craven God.

Jo grips the stick in her hand. She's seen many a film where monsters are killed by hurting the belly. She *knows* this is how it is done. Her sureness steeling her. She pushes herself through the pain, gets to her feet, and throws herself over the stump into the path of the arachnid God. She thrusts the point of the stick forward into the creatures belly and listens to the shriek of a deity unbound by circumstance. One so sure that it was to eat and kill the virgin Mary, that it never saw her coming.

The spider God falls, backwards into the fire, rolling out of it. Screeching in pain. "Mother," it shouts. "What are you doing?"

Jo scrambles after the thing. Her legs boiled and blistered, she is sure she can feel new things moving in there, free. More of them. More children. Bitter Gods to be birthed as hers.

She collapses over the spider, and pulls the stick from its belly, goo oozing from the wound, she brings it back and up, *Norma Bates the motherfucker*, and she stabs.

———

Daniel opens his eyes to her shriek again. "Fucking hell," he whispers to Steve. "You have to be kidding me." He moves to sit up but Steve stops him.

"She'll be fine," he mutters.

"Like fu—" Daniel's words are cut from the air as the blade from the knife slashes through the side of the tent. The sentence changes. "Jesus *Christ*."

Jo rips through the material. Blood dribbling from multiple wounds on her legs, clearly made from the knife, slicked in her own blood.

"Joey," Daniel screams, clambering over Steve to get to her as she bursts in through the side of the tent. "*Wake up!*"

Jo raises the knife like a serial killer and slashes it down towards Daniel. The tip of the blade sliding into his chest. Through the bone. Into his lung, bursting it. He grunts out in pain, first, then again as the stunned numbness takes him. She pulls the blade back and the two of them stand there for a split second. Everything quiet.

Serene.

Then he spits out a mouth of blood. His lungs filling with it. Drowning him. The lung collapsing. Breath hard to find.

Steve is on his knees. He's naked. Wide eyed. He's staring at Daniel. Dying there before him. He doesn't speak. He can't. He can't find words. Thought, even.

Jo pushes the blade into Daniel again, he grunts a third time and his knees drop away, he falls, slumps to the air mattress, blood squirting from him like a punctured balloon. Steve watches. Still. He mouths the word, what, before Jo falls on him. Her blood, flicking from her to him, her weight on top of him, he can do nothing but fall back. And she straddles him. Eyes full of anger and hate and fear. She brings the blade up.

"Please, don't," he says.

"Bastard child of mine," she screams. She slams the blade down, through his sternum, down then up, his blood spewing out. Down then up. The blood splashes over his face, into his mouth, warm and sticky. He watches. Helpless as Jo sticks him over and over like she's been paid to shank him in the shower. The heat of the tent, hotter with the blood, stench filling the space as Daniel makes hurring noises, unable to breathe through the waterfall of blood filling his lungs, his throat. Mouth.

Steve is surrounded by blackness. Surprised. He never thought it was going to end like this. His best friend murdering him and his lover in a mad rampage in the middle of the night. He's cold, but there is a warmth and a light and everything feels a little better.

Jo stabbing him, over and over. His torso becoming little more than chopped meat. Mince on a butcher's counter.

―――

Jo heaves air in as the spider stops moving. Rolls from its dead carcass, and to the ground, wet and sticky with its yellow bile blood.

But as she lay there she can still feel them moving

about inside her. Spiders don't lay one egg, do they? And she can't let them escape. She can't birth them. They will be an army of Gods unbeatable. Rampant. *Rampaging*.

She pushes herself to sit. Sees the movement in her legs. She takes the stick and stabs into her flesh. Missed it. But she twists the blade, destroying the pathway it was using. *Yes*. That's it. Destroy the pathways and trap them inside her. Until there is nowhere left for them to run. Then she can get them. Trapped inside her.

Jo giggles as she puts the plan into motion. She stabs at the movement, not concerned if she misses. Stabs the blade into her flesh again. A different one. There under the skin.

One in her leg.

One under the skin of her stomach.

The other leg.

She keeps stabbing and twisting.

She has got to catch them all.

About the Author

Ash is a British horror author. He resides in the south, in the Garden of England. He writes horror that is sometimes fantastical, sometimes grounded, but always deeply graphic, and black with humour.

www.ashericmore.com

Printed in Great Britain
by Amazon